JiMMY SNiFFLES
Double Trouble

D1460347

Librarian Reviewer
Katharine Kan
Graphic novel reviewer and Library Consultant, Panama City, FL
MLS in Library and Information Studies, University of Hawaii at
Manoa, HI

Reading Consultant
Elizabeth Stedem
Educator/Consultant, Colorado Springs, CO
MA in Elementary Education, University of Denver, CO

STONE ARCH BOOKS
MINNEAPOLIS   SAN DIEGO

Graphic Sparks are published by Stone Arch Books,
A Capstone Imprint
151 Good Counsel Drive, P.O. Box 669,
Mankato, Minnesota 56002.
www.capstonepub.com

Library of Congress Cataloging-in-Publication Data
Nickel, Scott.
　　Double Trouble / by Scott Nickel; illustrated by Steve Harpster.
　　p. cm. — (Graphic Sparks. Jimmy Sniffles)
　　ISBN-13: 978-1-59889-314-4 (library binding)
　　ISBN-10: 1-59889-314-9 (library binding)
　　ISBN-13: 978-1-59889-411-0 (paperback)
　　ISBN-10: 1-59889-411-0(paperback)
　　1. Graphic novels. I. Harpster, Steve. II. Title.
PN6727.N544D68 2007
741.5'973—dc22   2006028025

Summary: Jimmy Sniffles' archenemy, the creepy Dr. Von Snotenstein, devises a truly
stinky plan. He creates an evil twin from a single hair of Jimmy's nose. Then he gives the
new Jimmy Two more powers than our favorite Super Sneezer. Good versus evil in a literal
nose-to-nose battle!

Art Director: Heather Kindseth
Graphic Designer: Brann Garvey

Printed in the United States of America in Stevens Point, Wisconsin.
082015
009141R

Jimmy Sniffles

Double Trouble

by Scott Nickel
illustrated by Steve Harpster

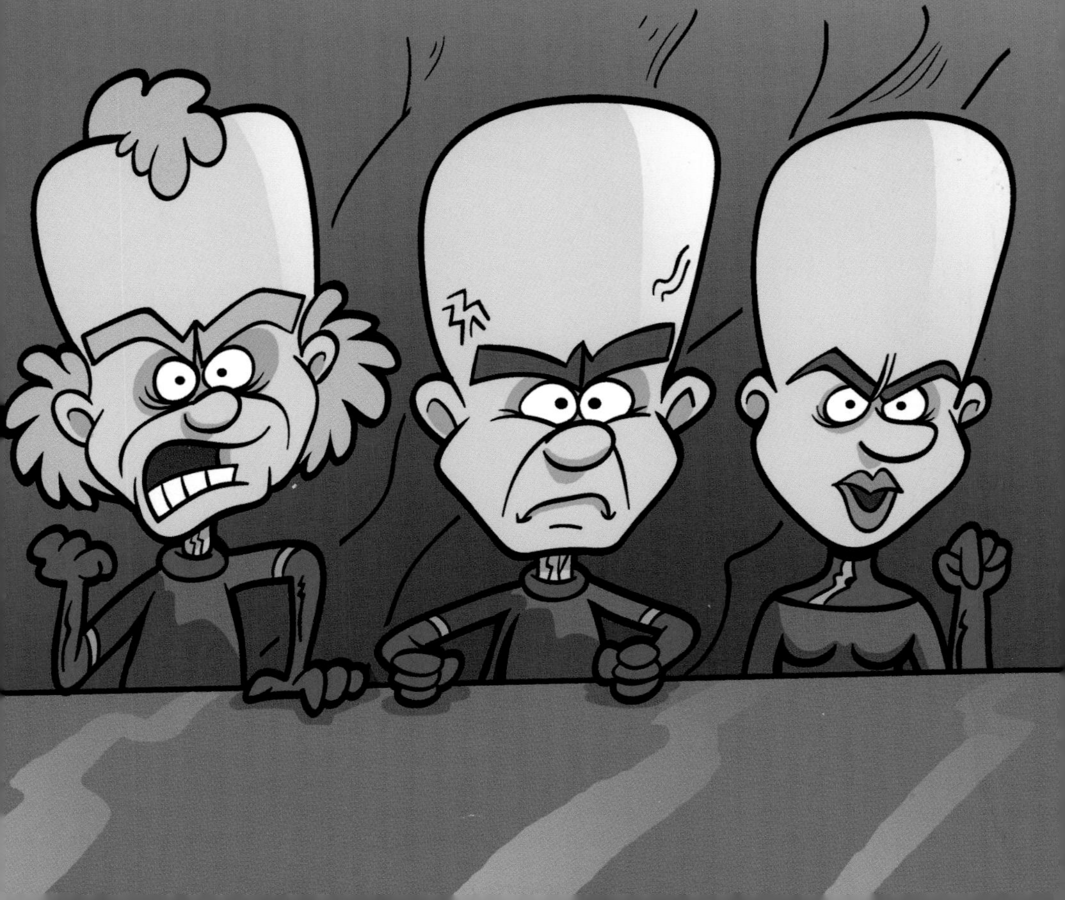

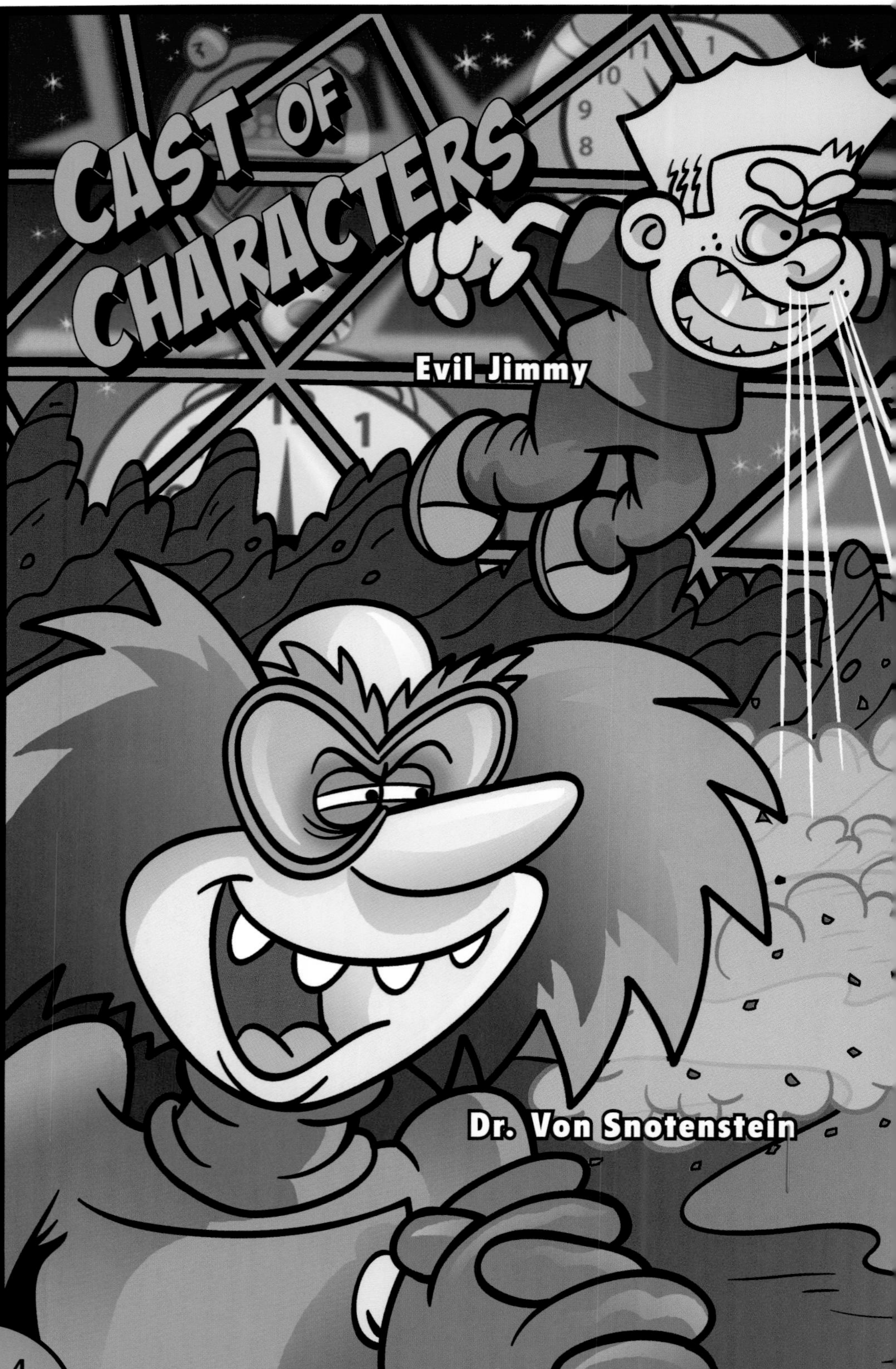
CAST OF CHARACTERS
Evil Jimmy
Dr. Von Snotenstein

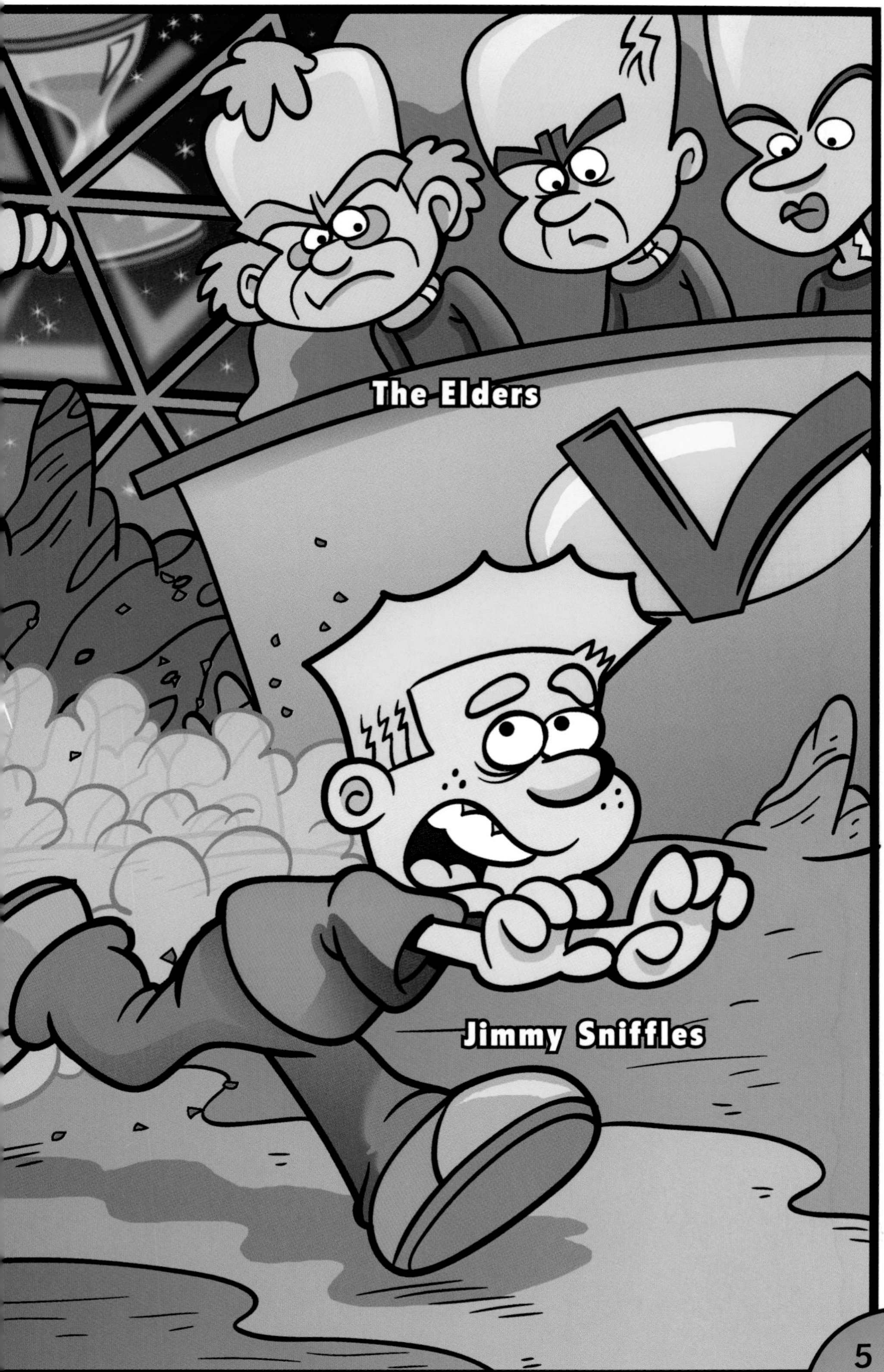
The Elders
Jimmy Sniffles

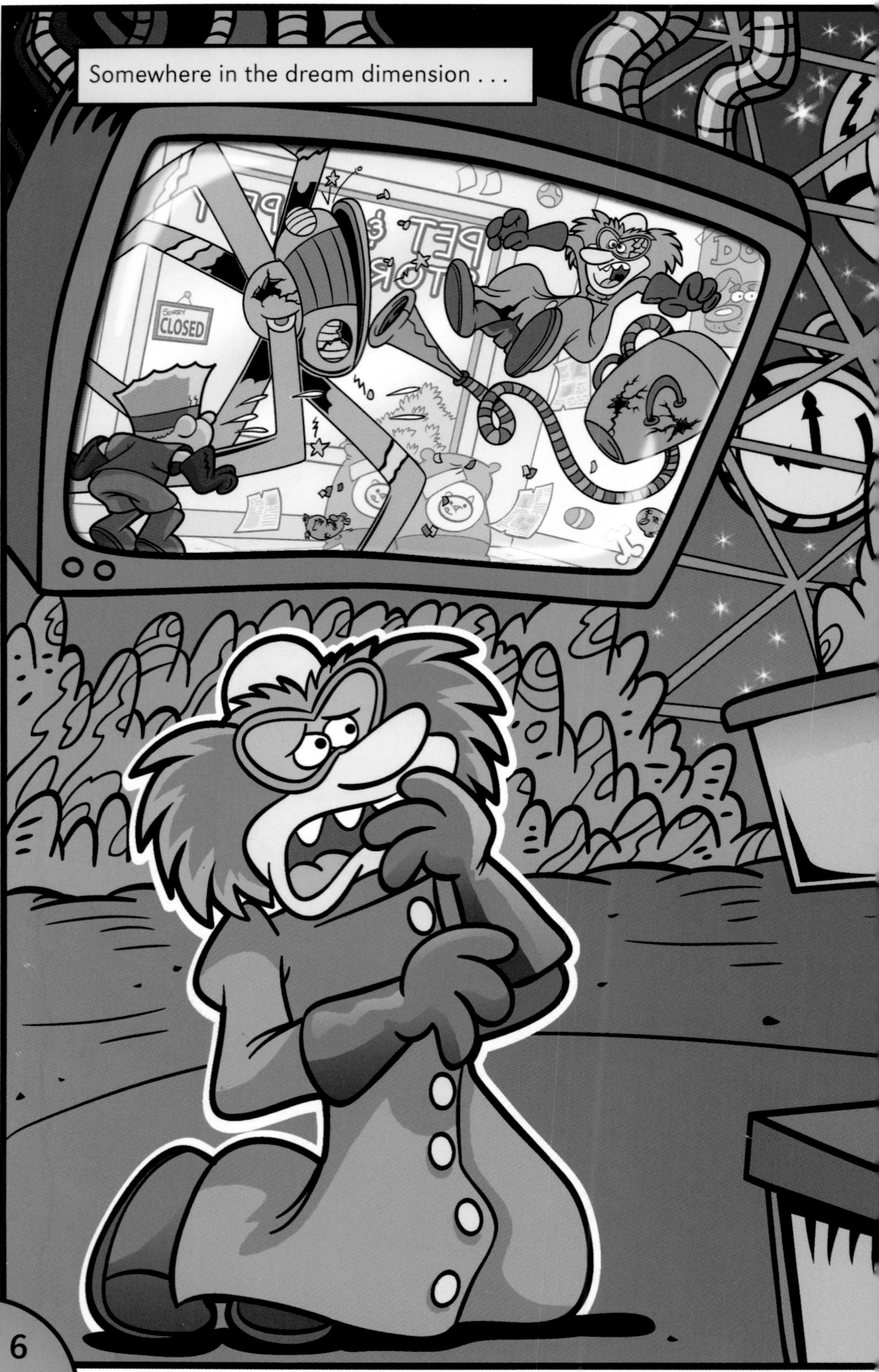
Somewhere in the dream dimension . . .
SORRY
CLOSED
PET

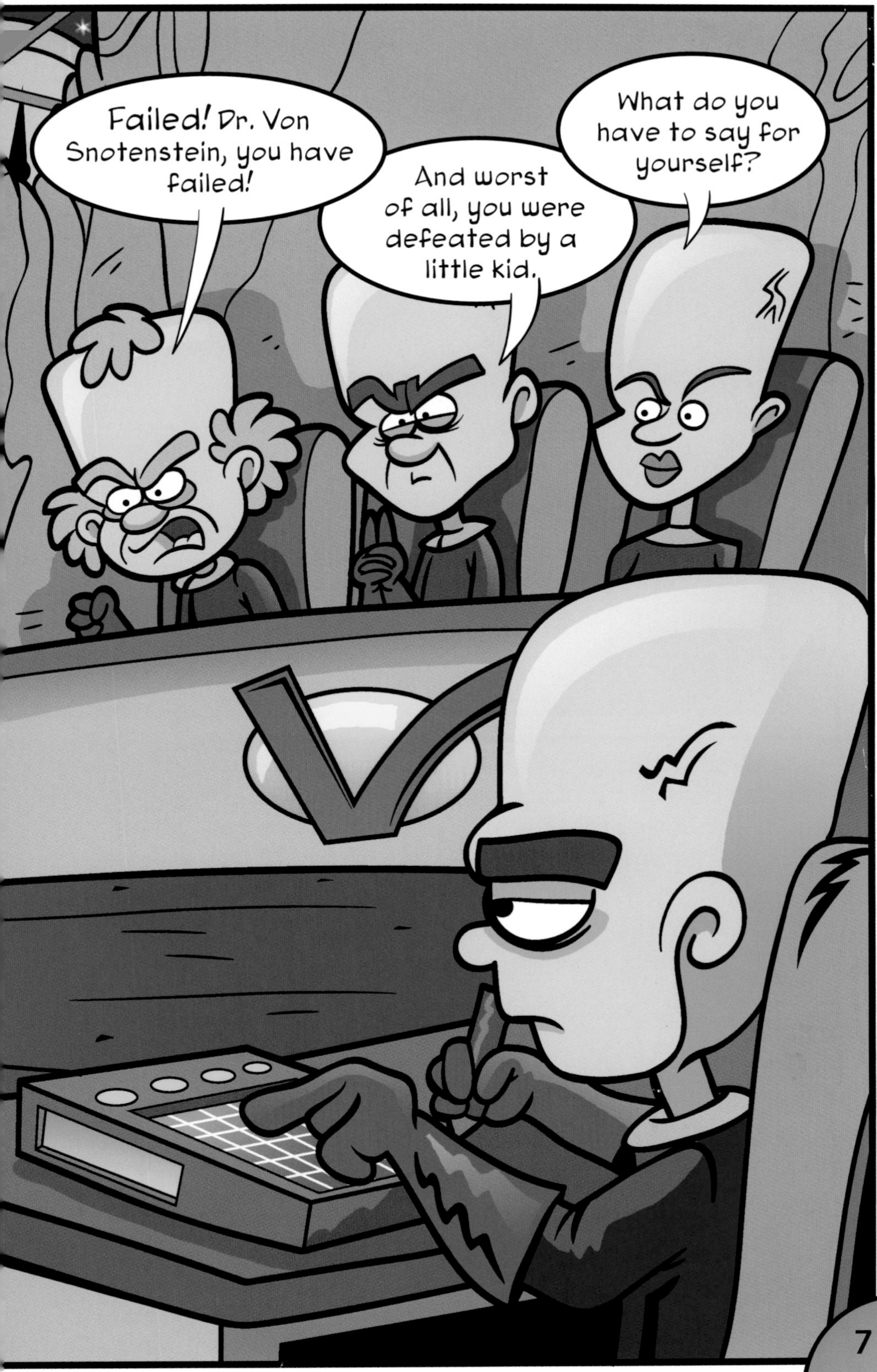
Failed! Dr. Von Snotenstein, you have failed!
And worst of all, you were defeated by a little kid.
What do you have to say for yourself?

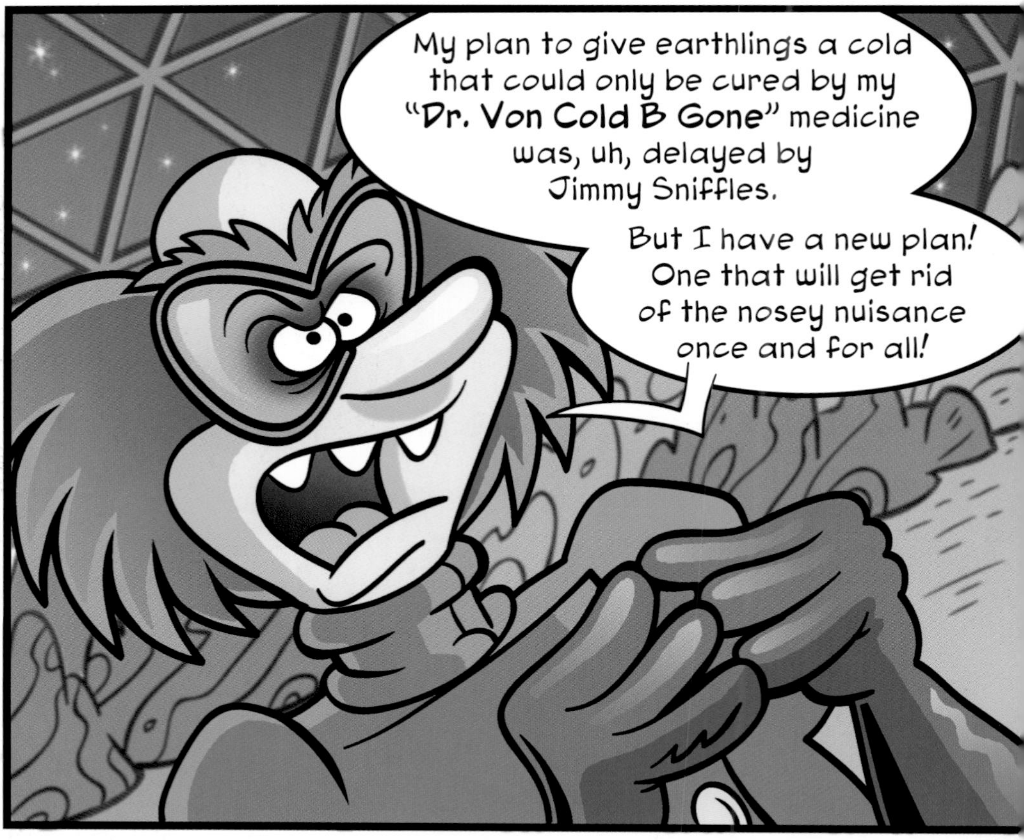
My plan to give earthlings a cold that could only be cured by my "**Dr. Von Cold B Gone**" medicine was, uh, delayed by Jimmy Sniffles.
But I have a new plan! One that will get rid of the nosey nuisance once and for all!

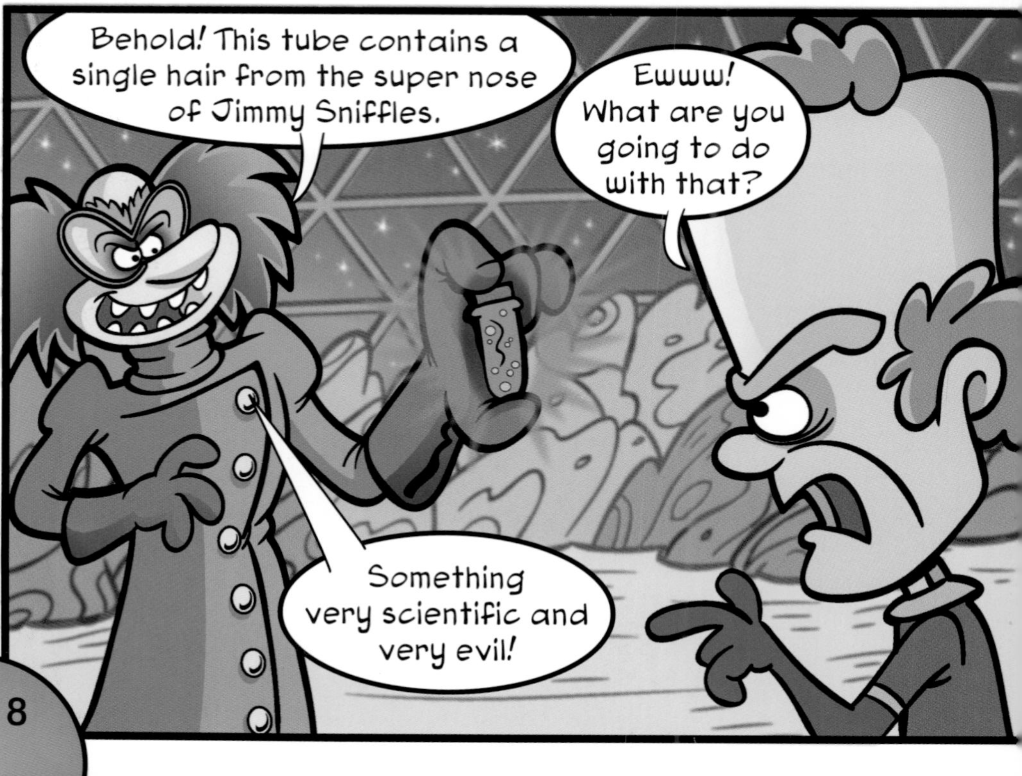
Behold! This tube contains a single hair from the super nose of Jimmy Sniffles.
Ewww! What are you going to do with that?
Something very scientific and very evil!

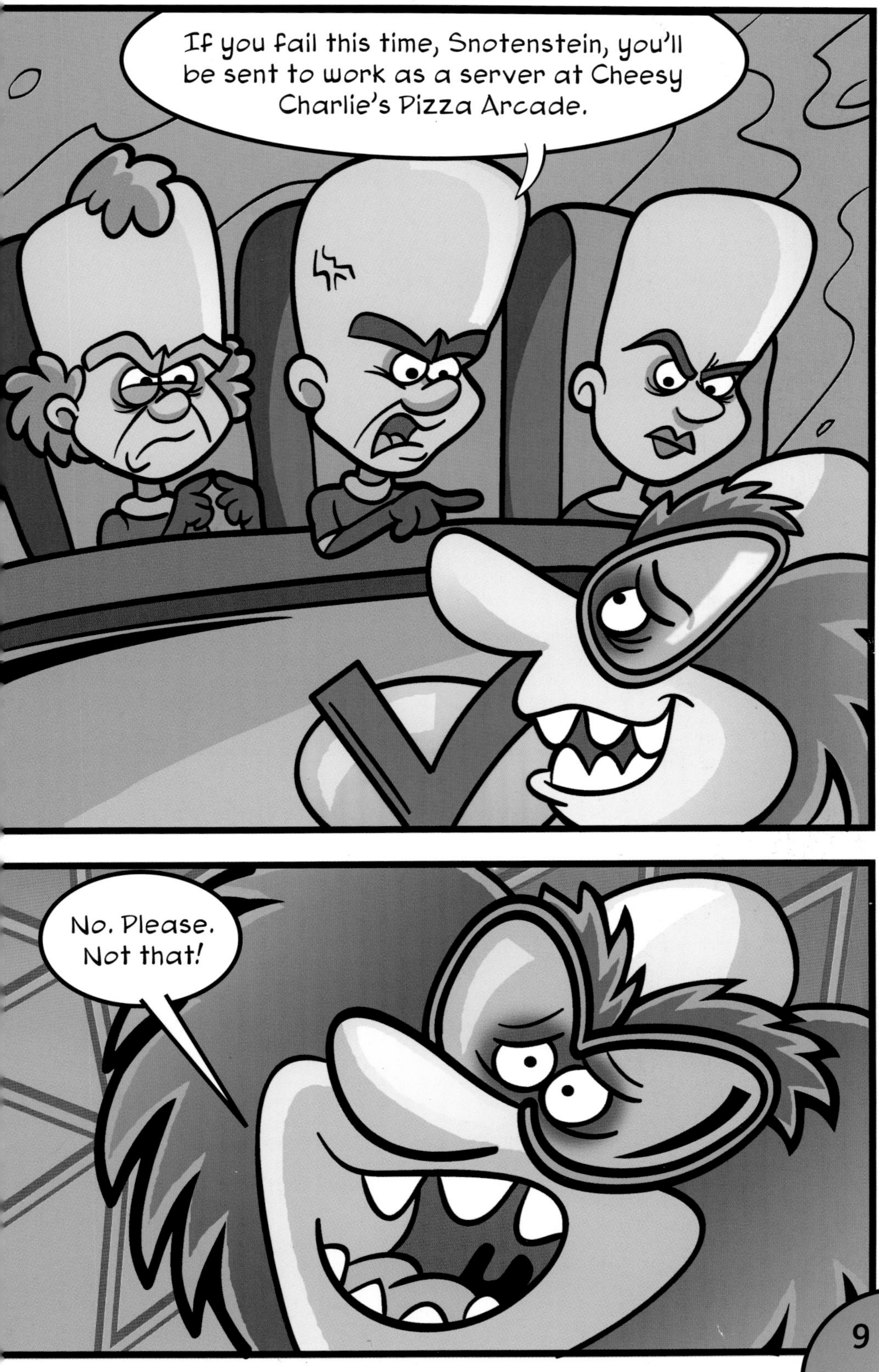
If you fail this time, Snotenstein, you'll be sent to work as a server at Cheesy Charlie's Pizza Arcade.
No. Please. Not that!

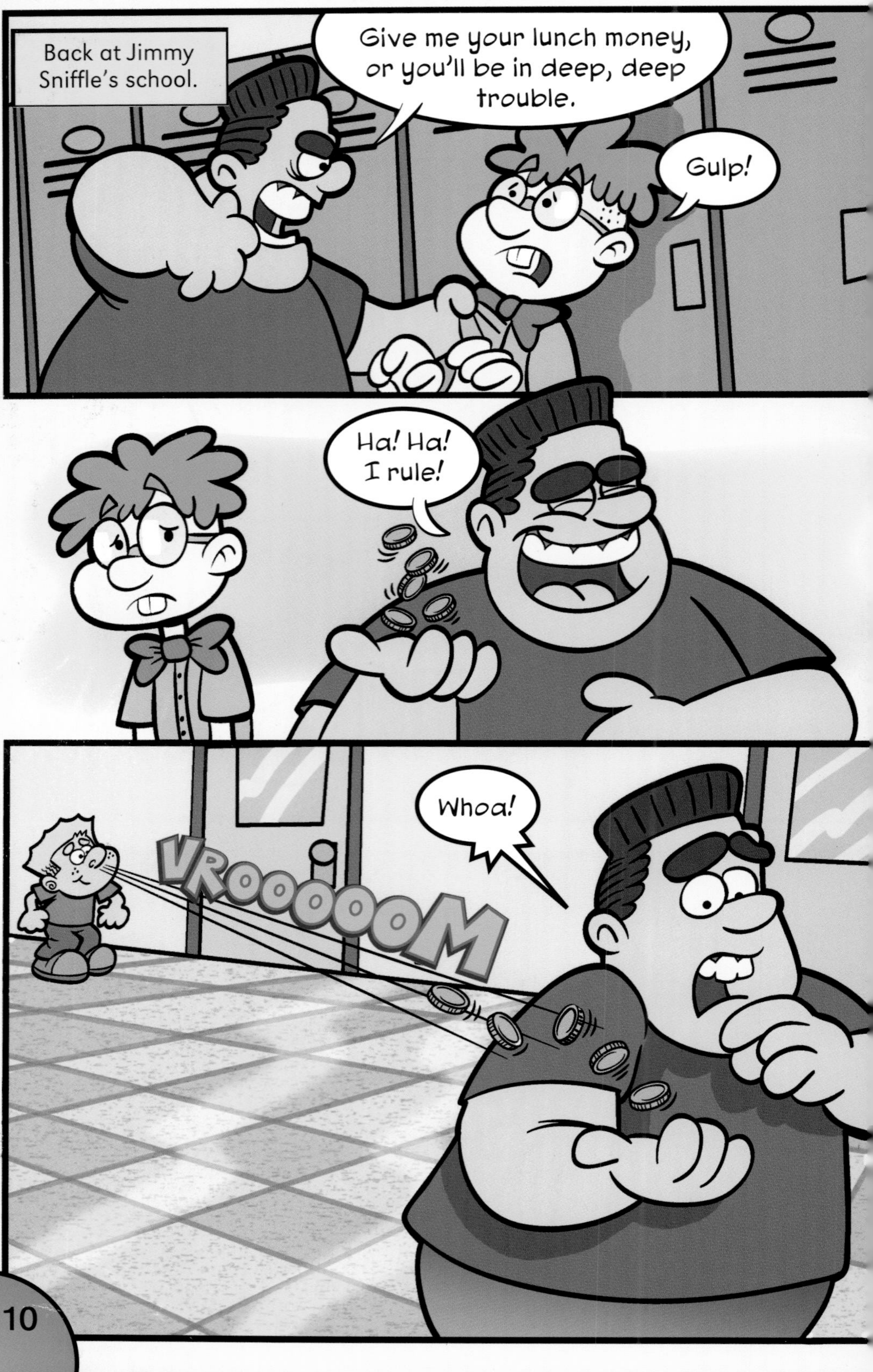
Back at Jimmy Sniffle's school.
Give me your lunch money, or you'll be in deep, deep trouble.
Gulp!
Ha! Ha! I rule!
Whoa!
VROOOOOOM

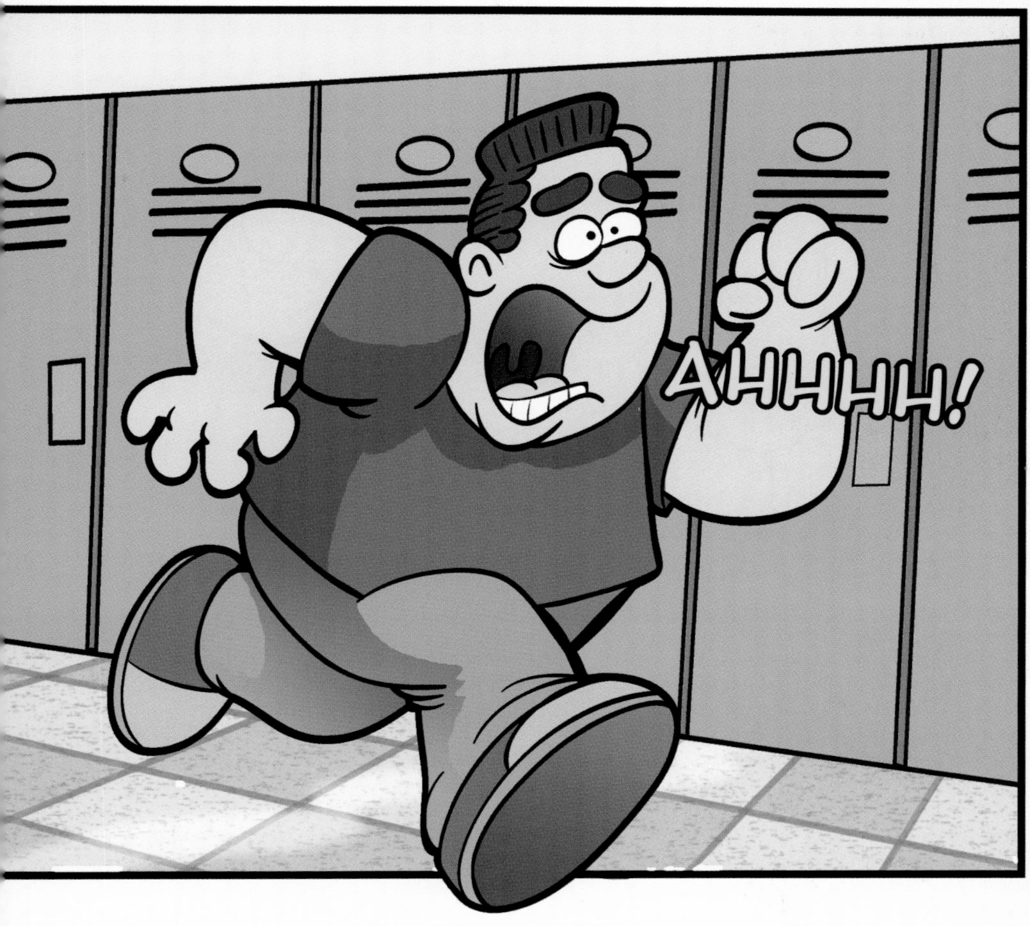
AHHHHH!

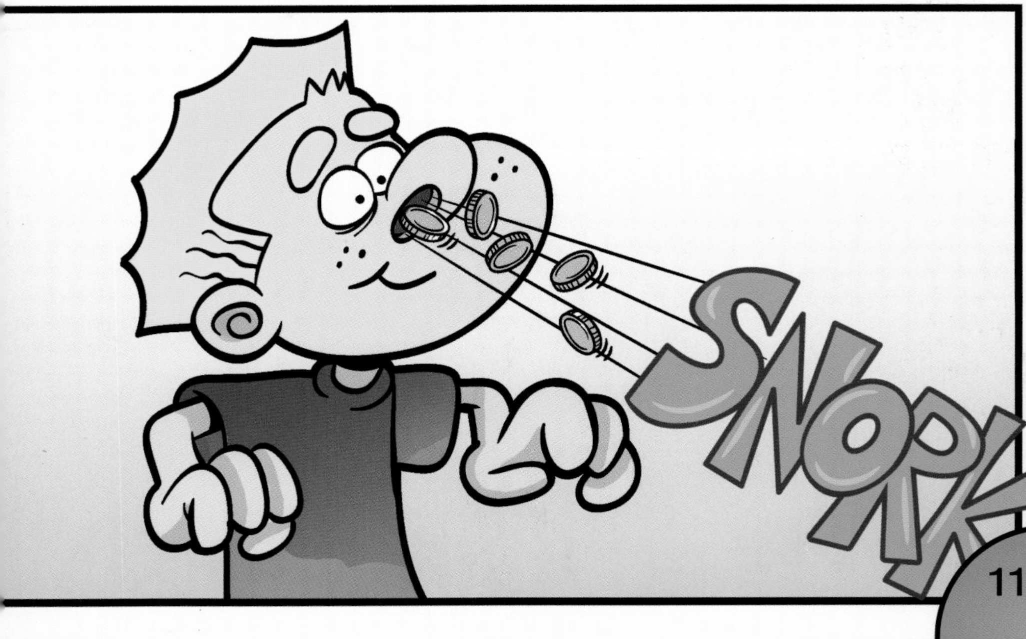
SNORK!

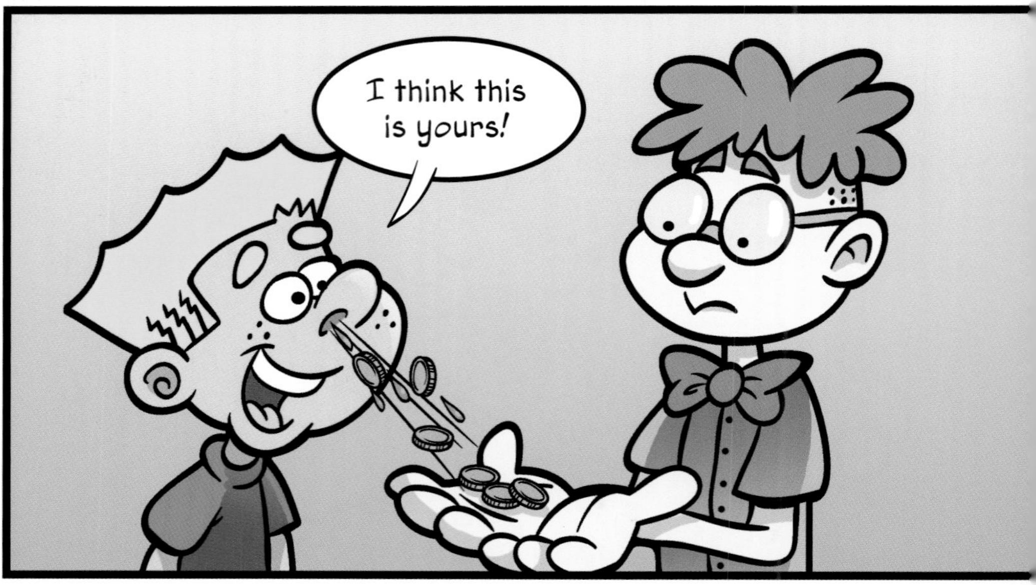
I think this is yours!

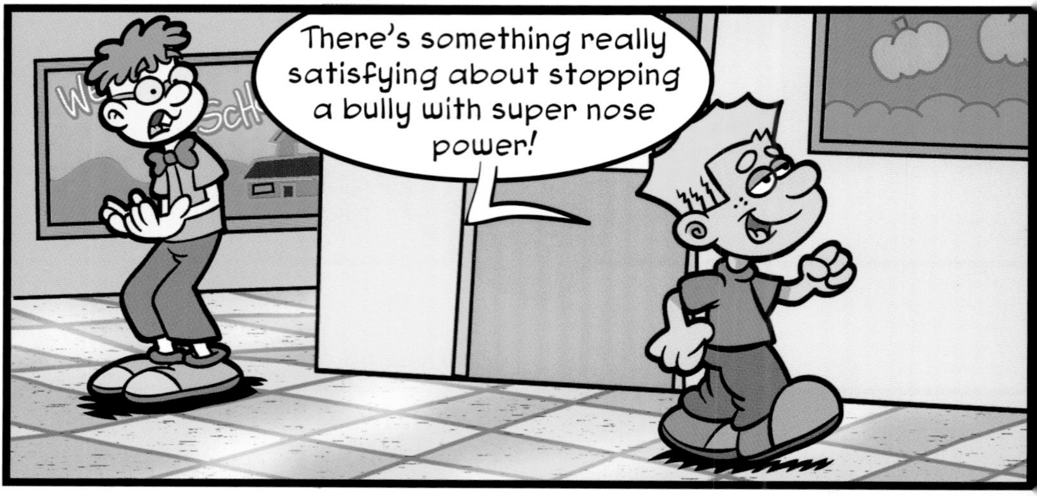
There's something really satisfying about stopping a bully with super nose power!

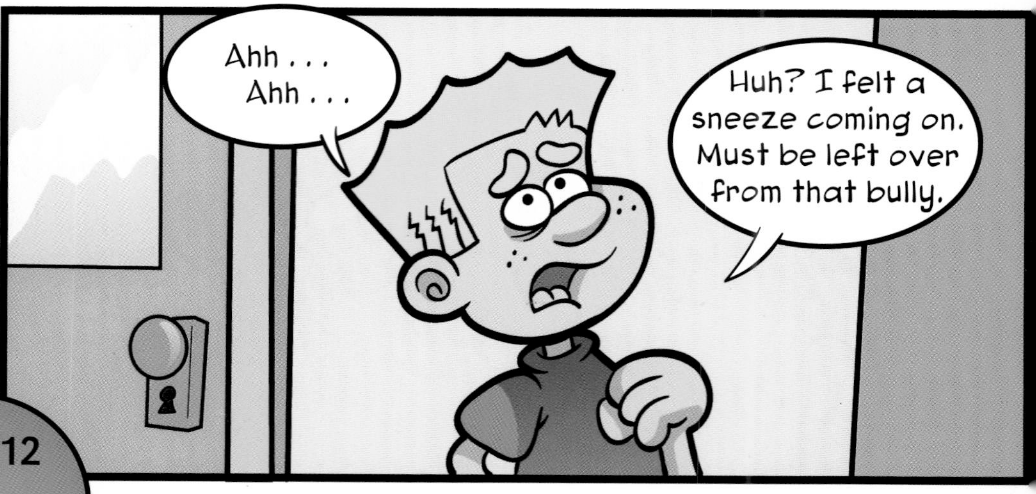
Ahh . . .
Ahh . . .
Huh? I felt a sneeze coming on. Must be left over from that bully.

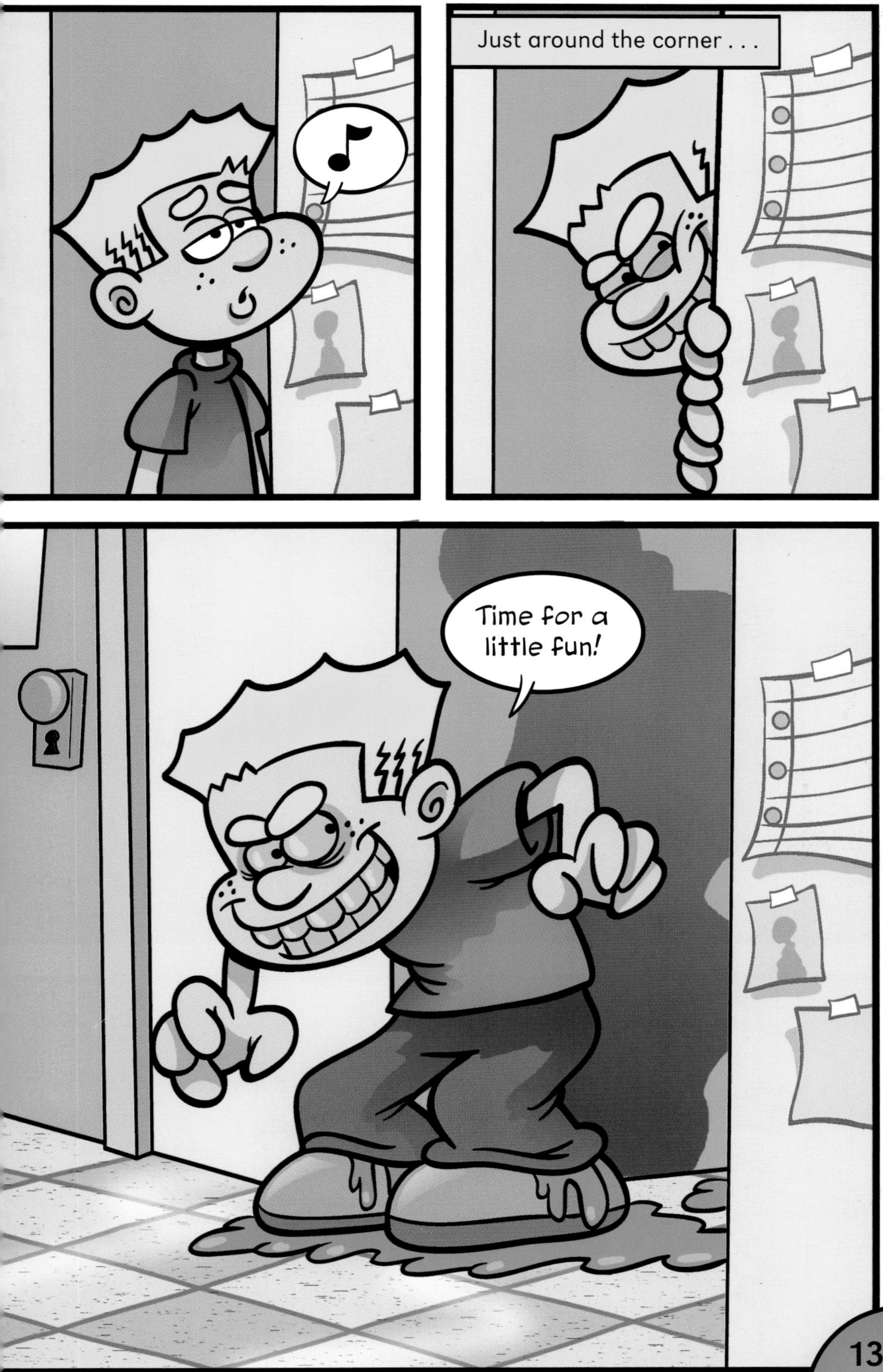
Just around the corner . . .
Time for a little fun!

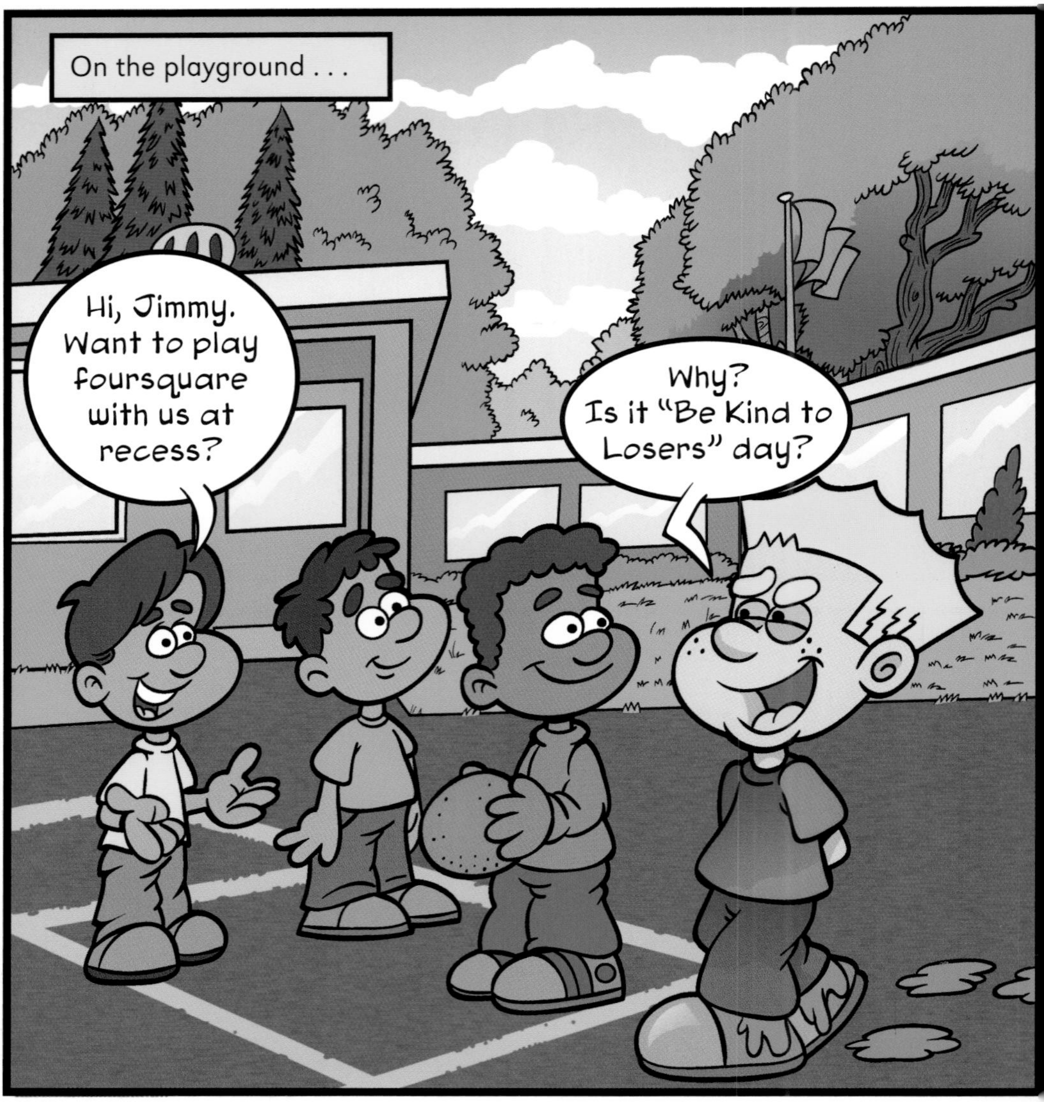
On the playground . . .
Hi, Jimmy. Want to play foursquare with us at recess?
Why? Is it "Be Kind to Losers" day?

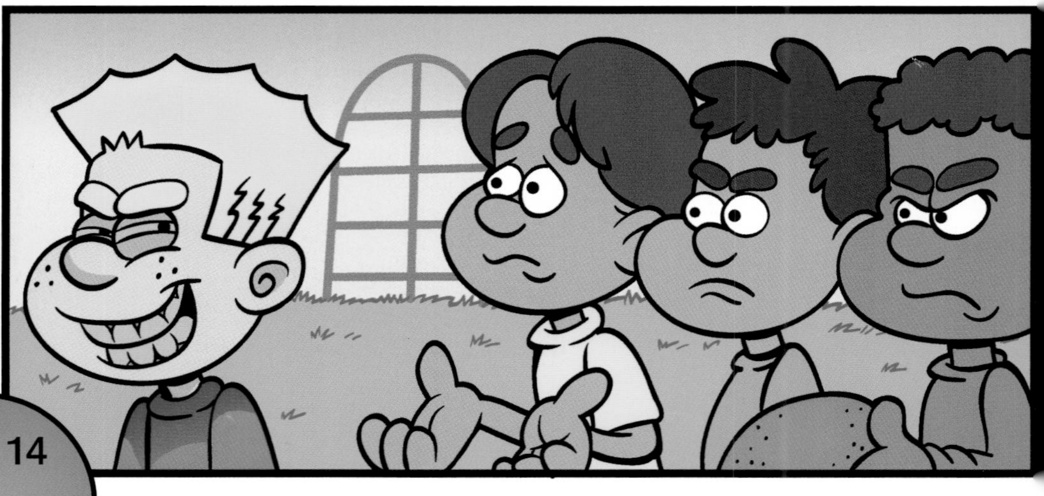

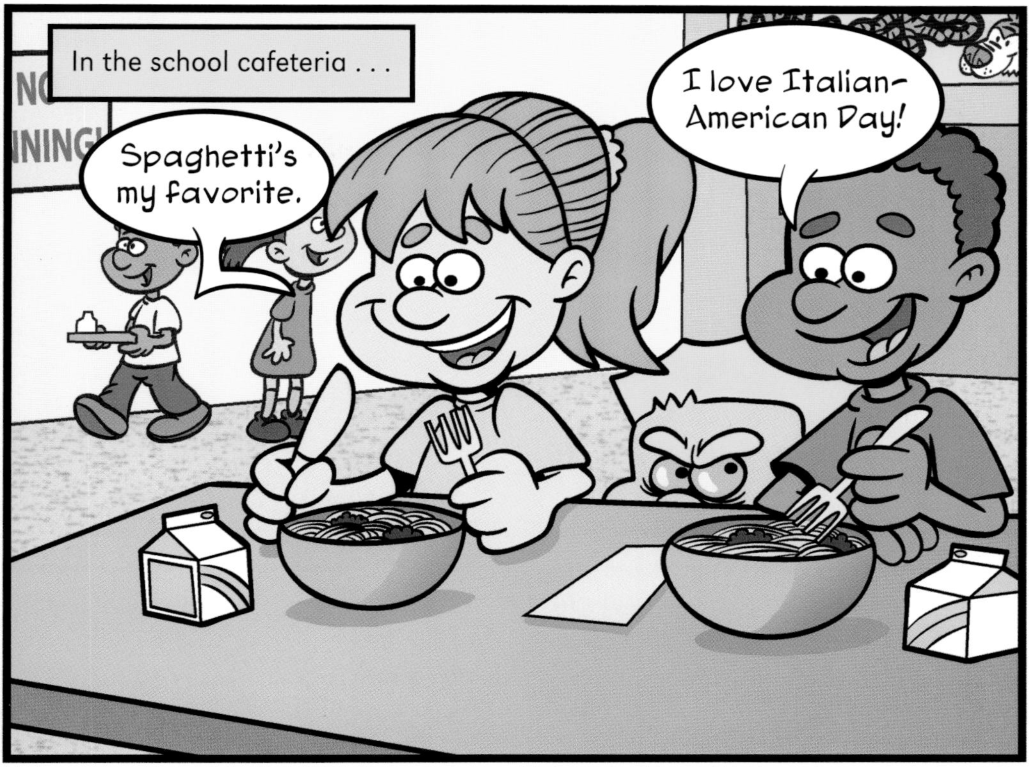
In the school cafeteria . . .
Spaghetti's my favorite.
I love Italian-American Day!

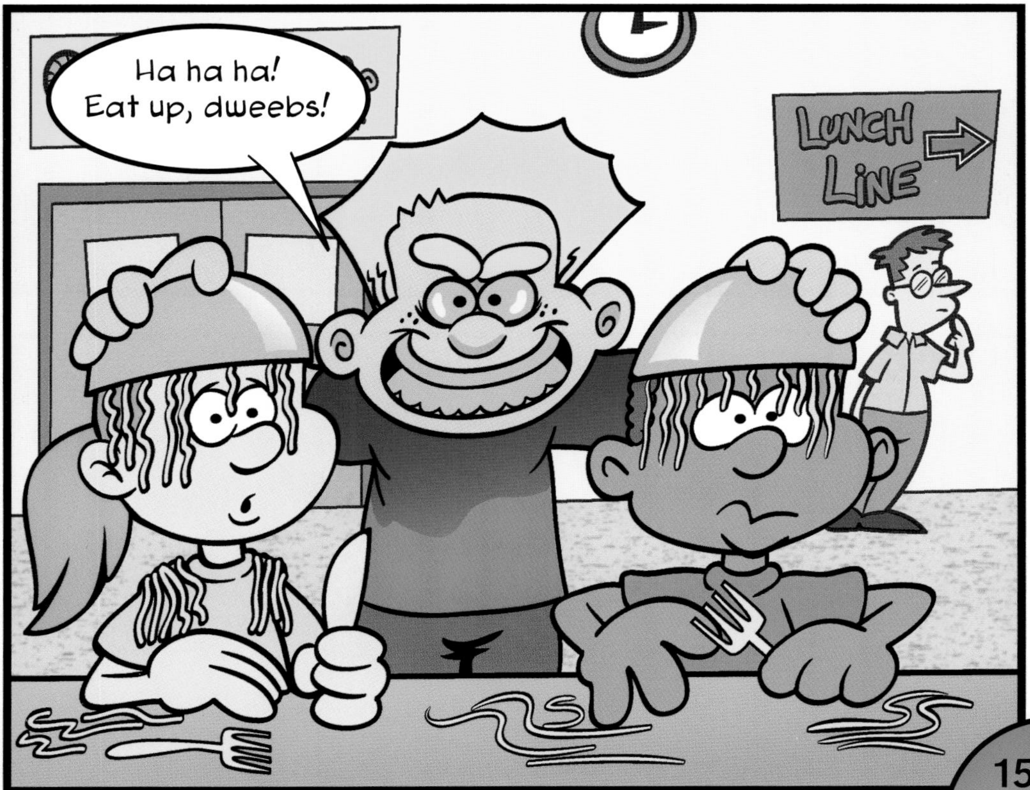
Ha ha ha! Eat up, dweebs!
LUNCH LINE

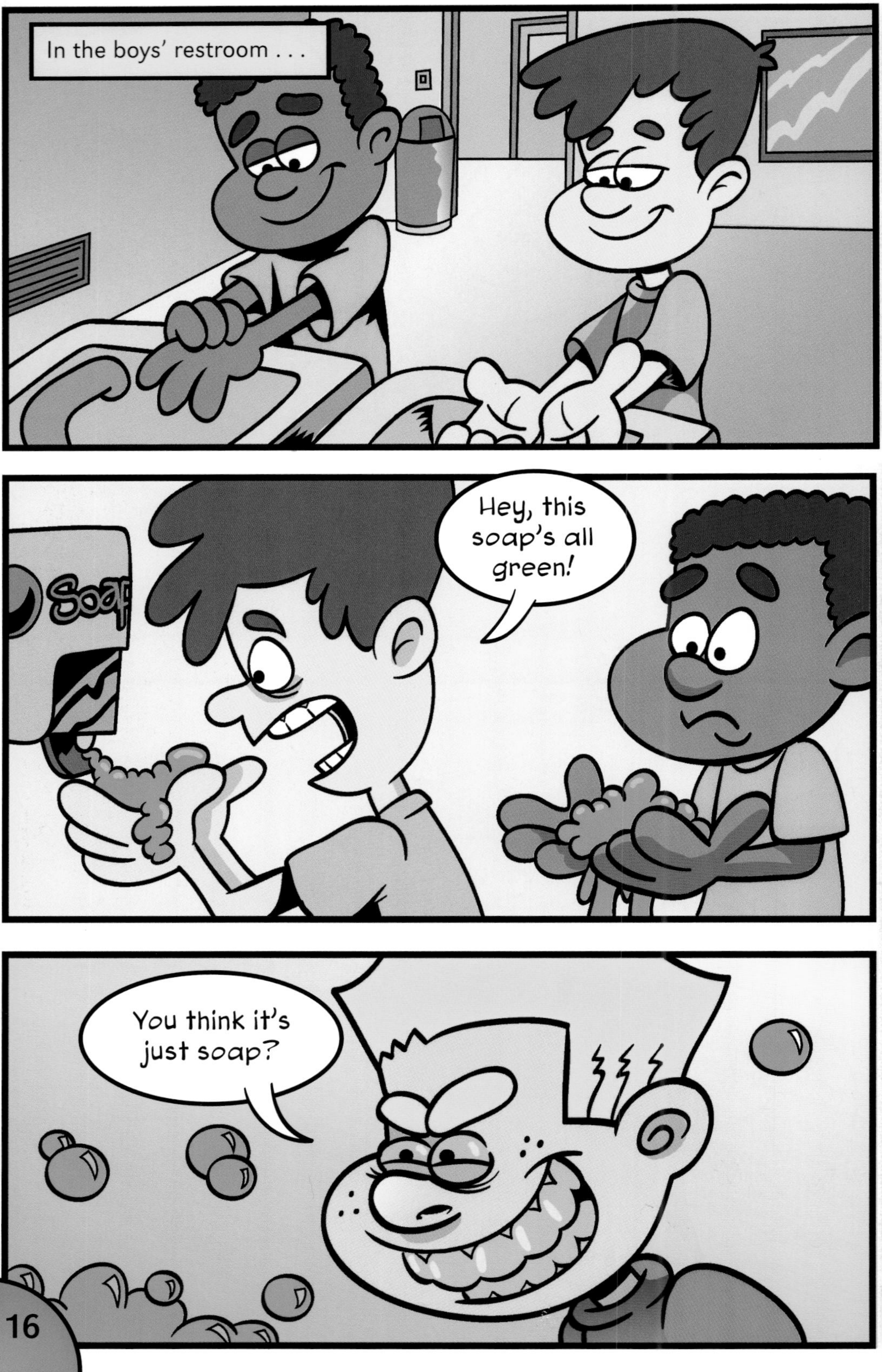
In the boys' restroom . . .
Hey, this soap's all green!
Soap
You think it's just soap?

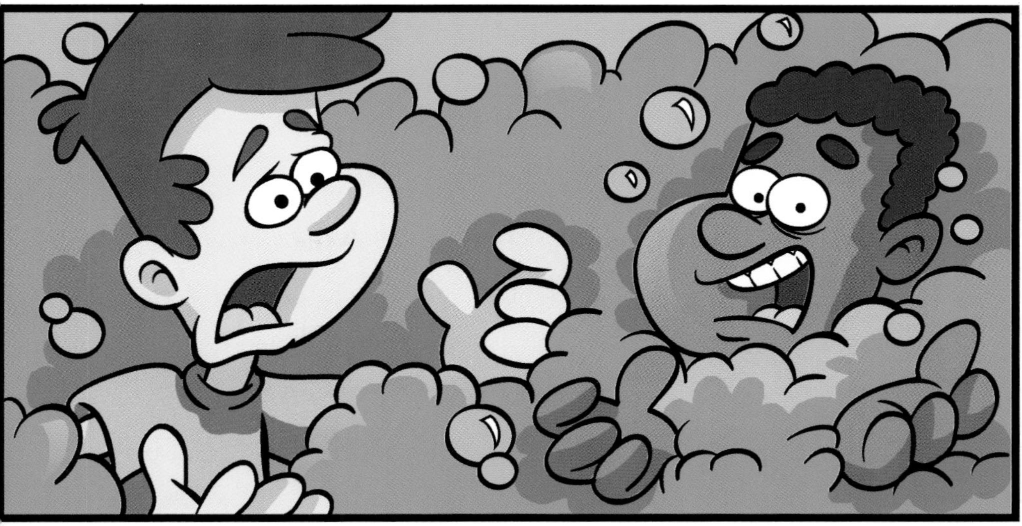

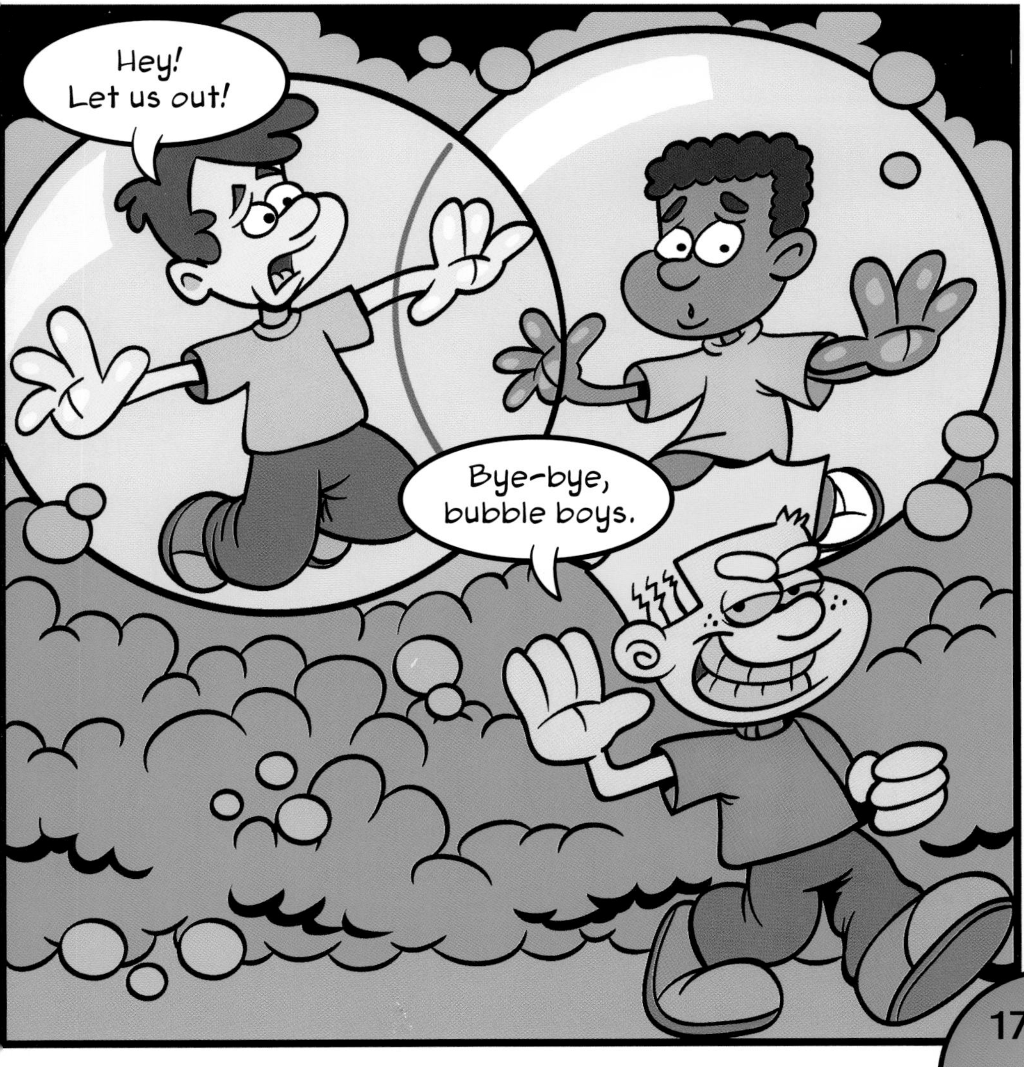
Hey!
Let us out!
Bye-bye,
bubble boys.

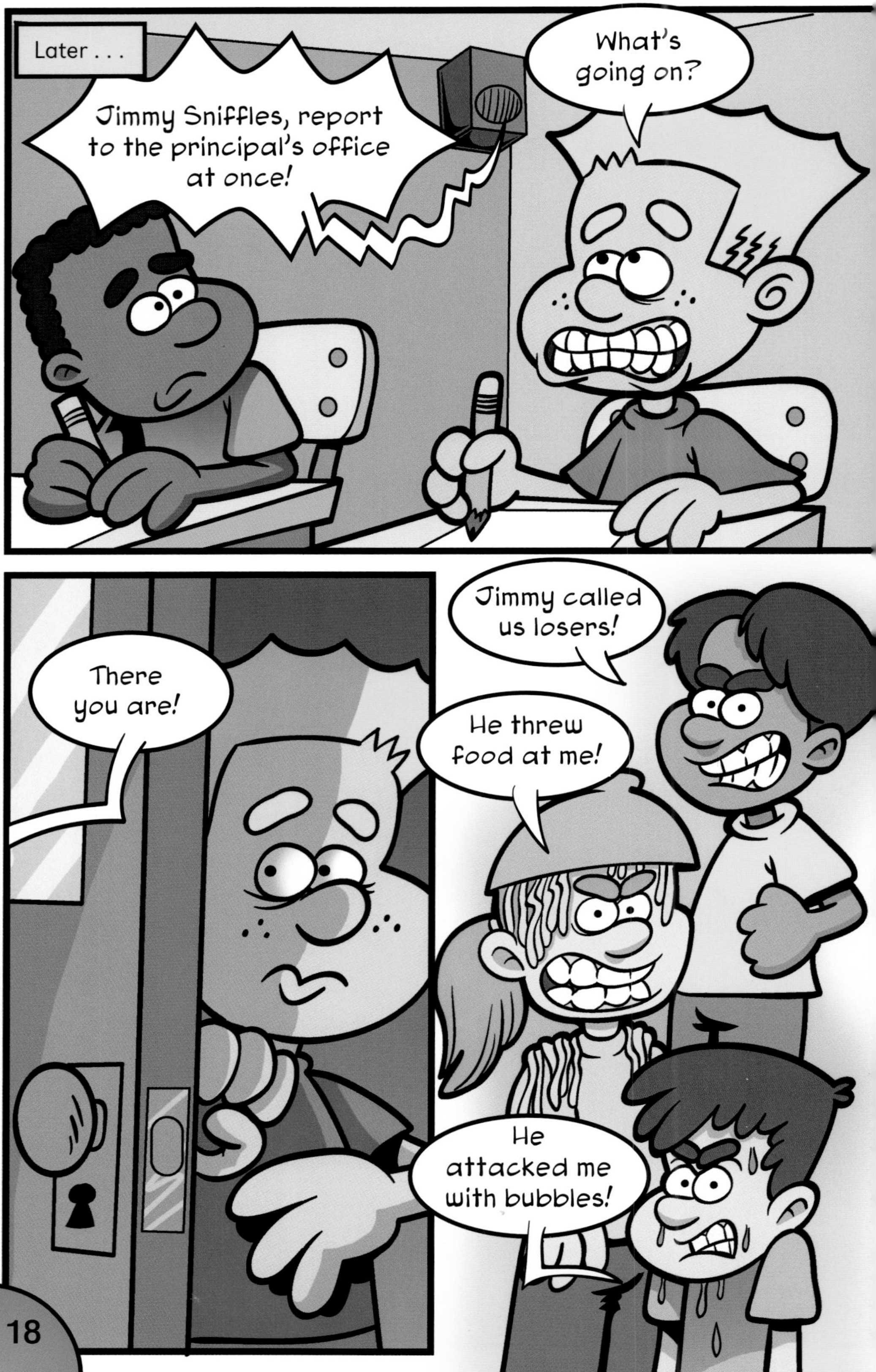
Later . . .
Jimmy Sniffles, report to the principal's office at once!
What's going on?
There you are!
Jimmy called us losers!
He threw food at me!
He attacked me with bubbles!

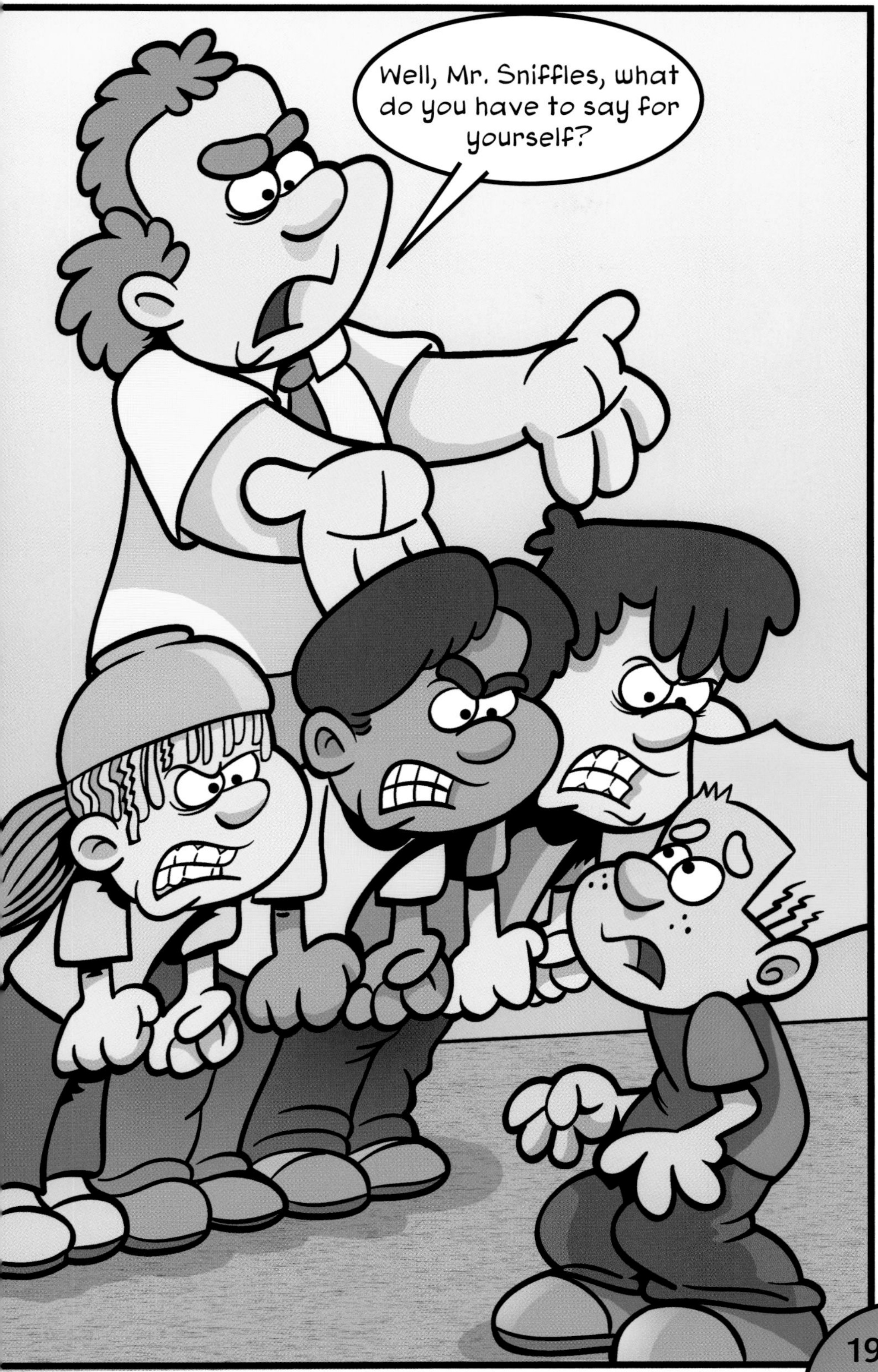
Well, Mr. Sniffles, what do you have to say for yourself?

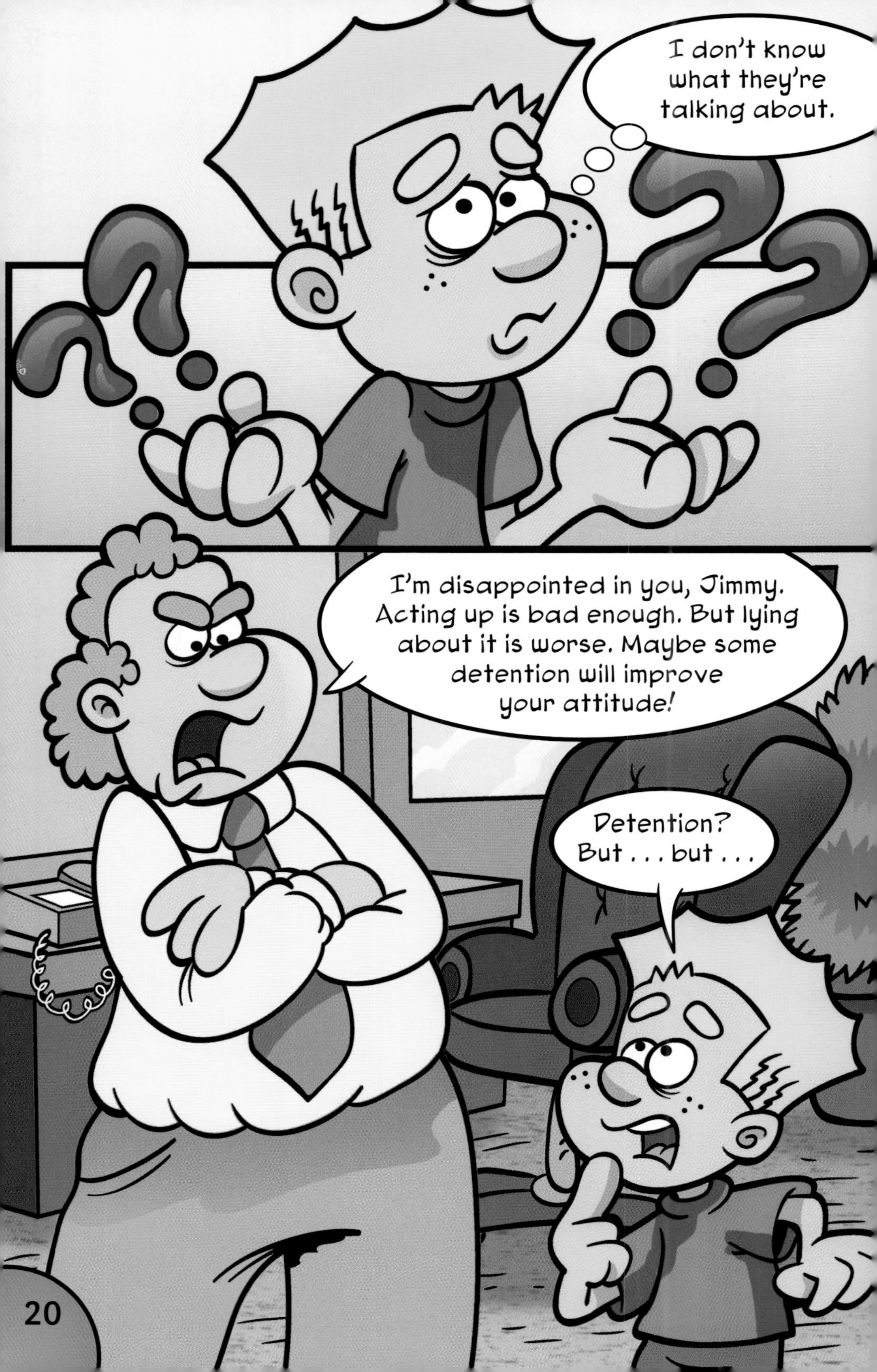
I don't know what they're talking about.
I'm disappointed in you, Jimmy. Acting up is bad enough. But lying about it is worse. Maybe some detention will improve your attitude!
Detention? But . . . but . . .

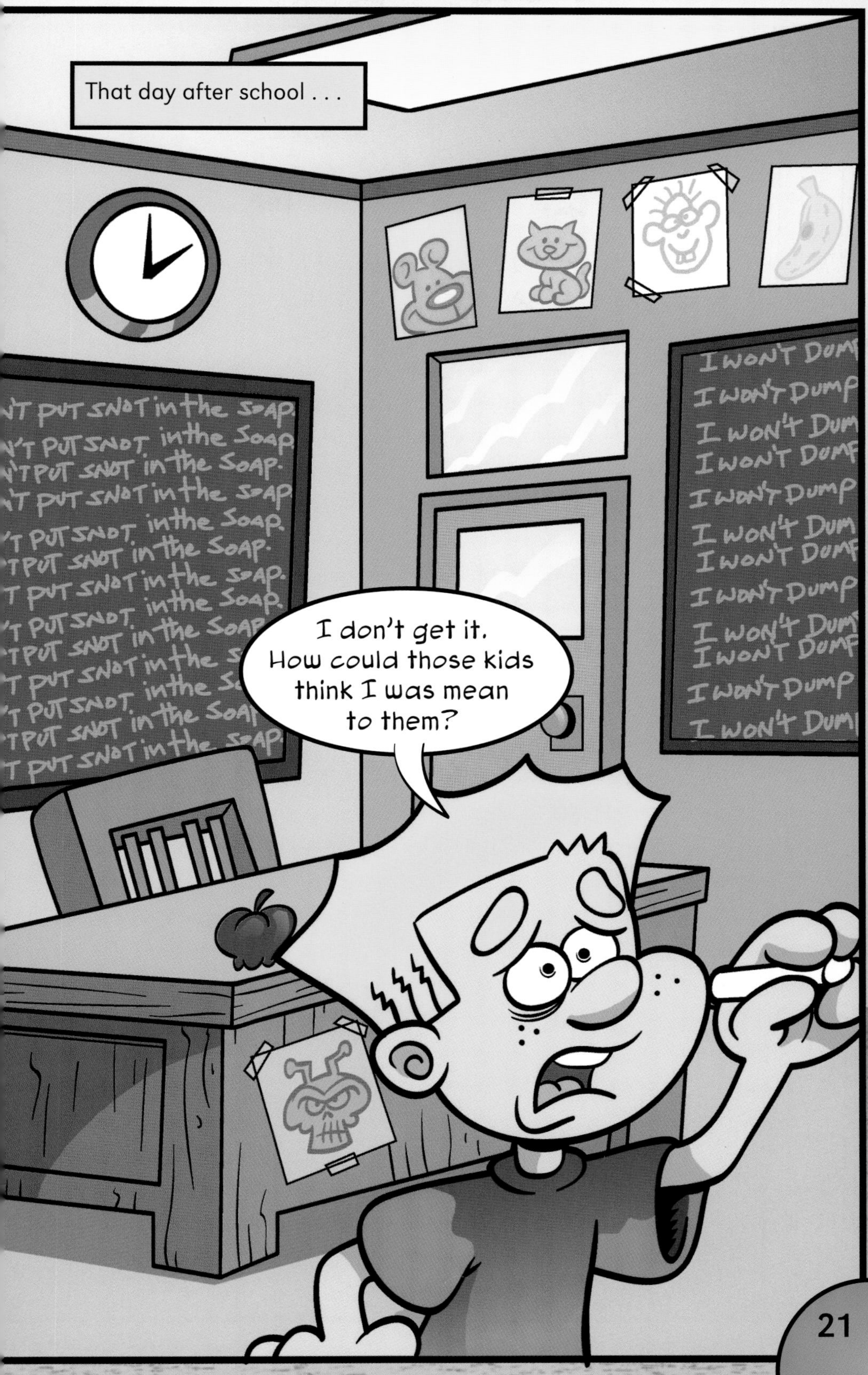
That day after school . . .
I don't get it. How could those kids think I was mean to them?

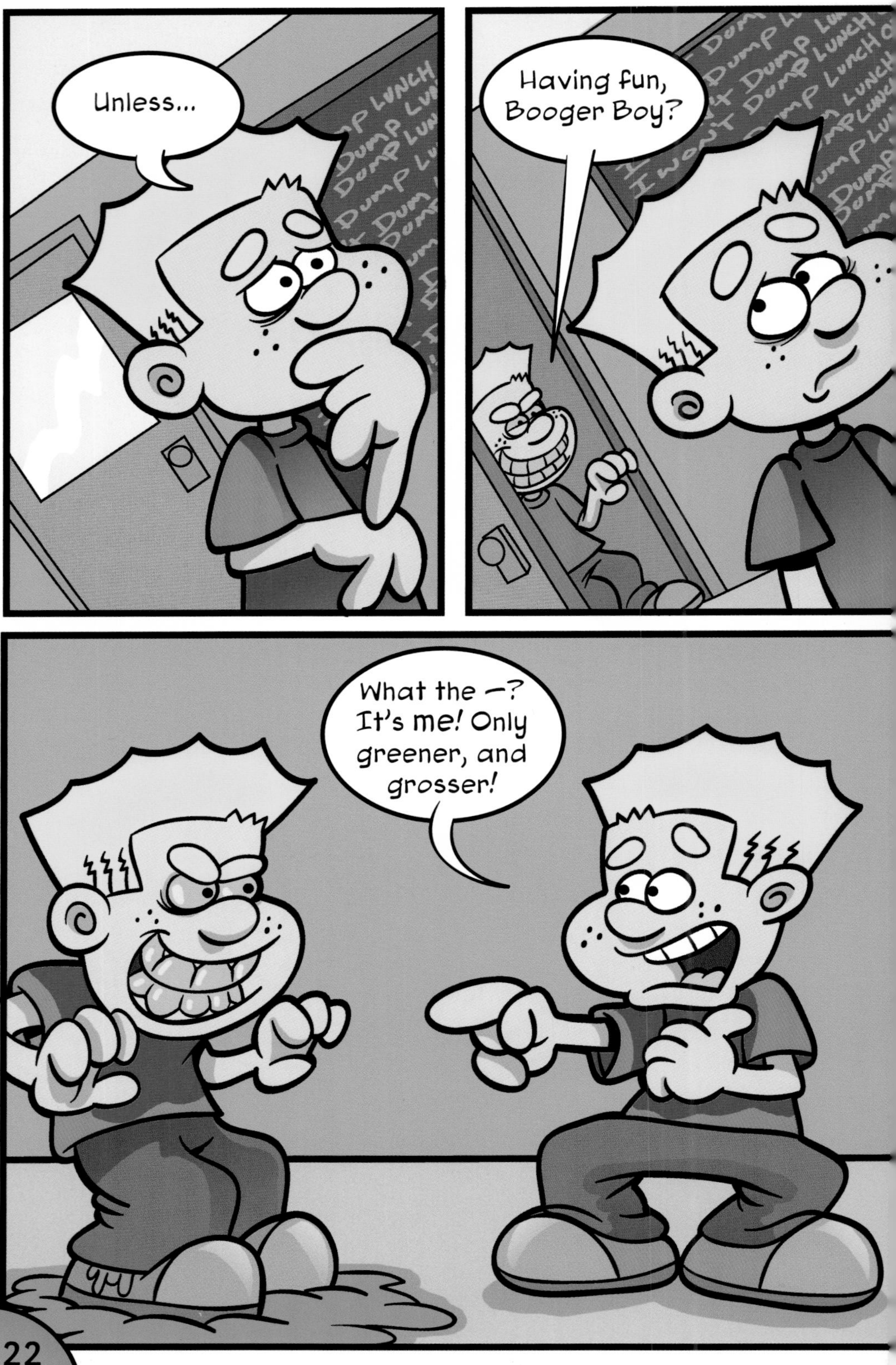
Unless...
Having fun, Booger Boy?
What the –? It's me! Only greener, and grosser!

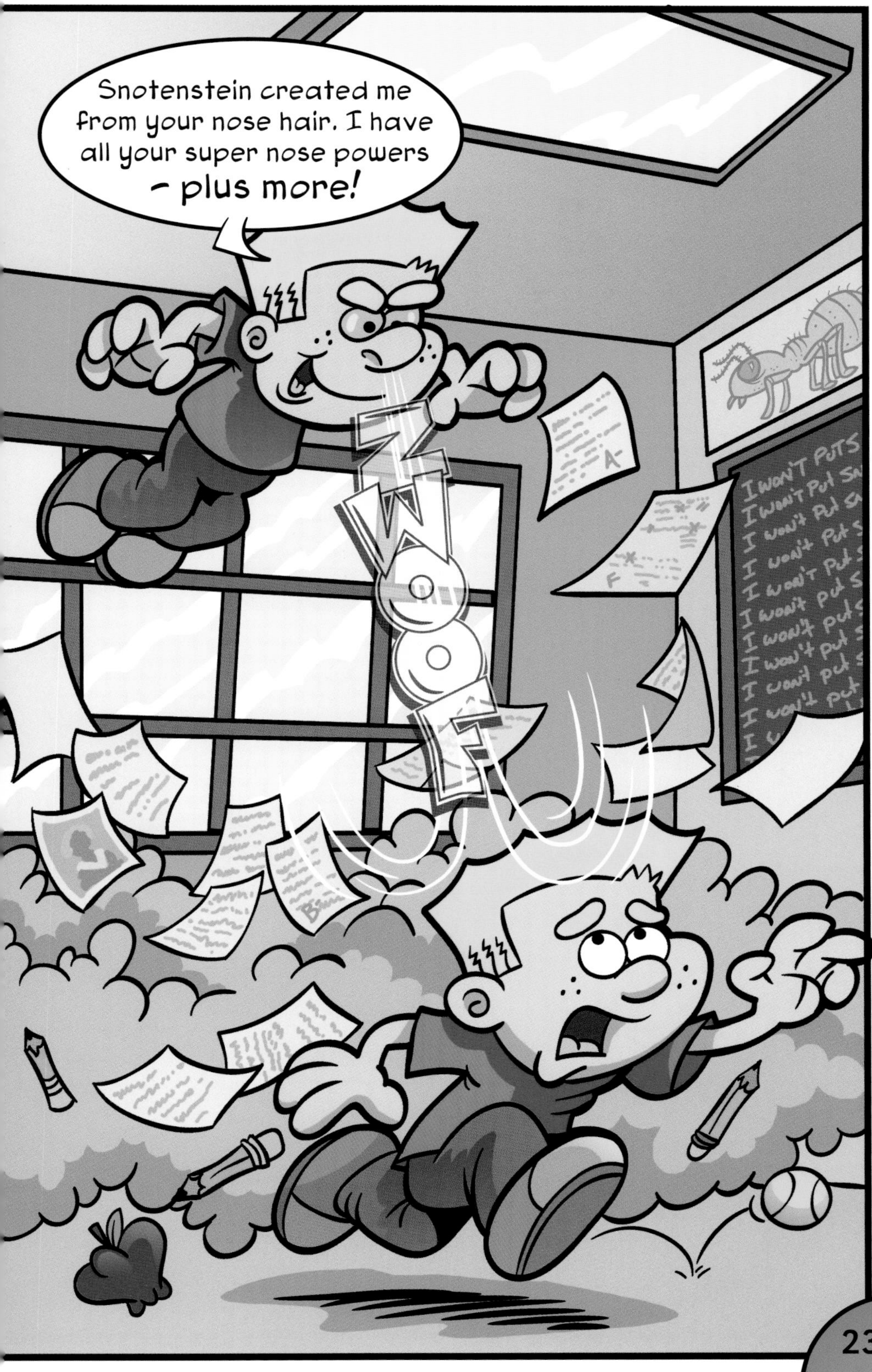
Snotenstein created me from your nose hair. I have all your super nose powers – plus more!
ZWOOF
I WON'T PUT S
I won't put S

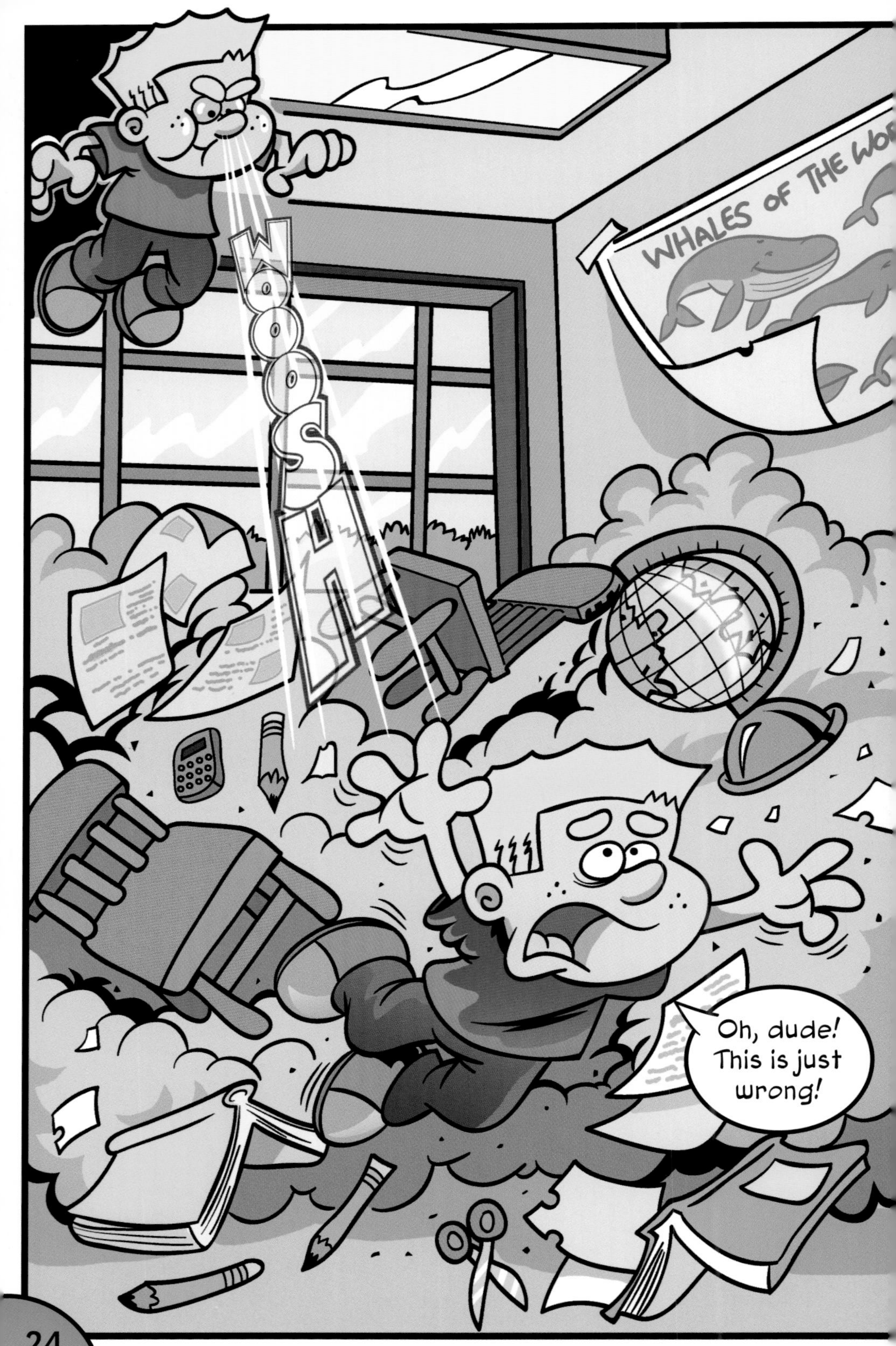
WHALES OF THE WO
WOOOSH
Oh, dude! This is just wrong!

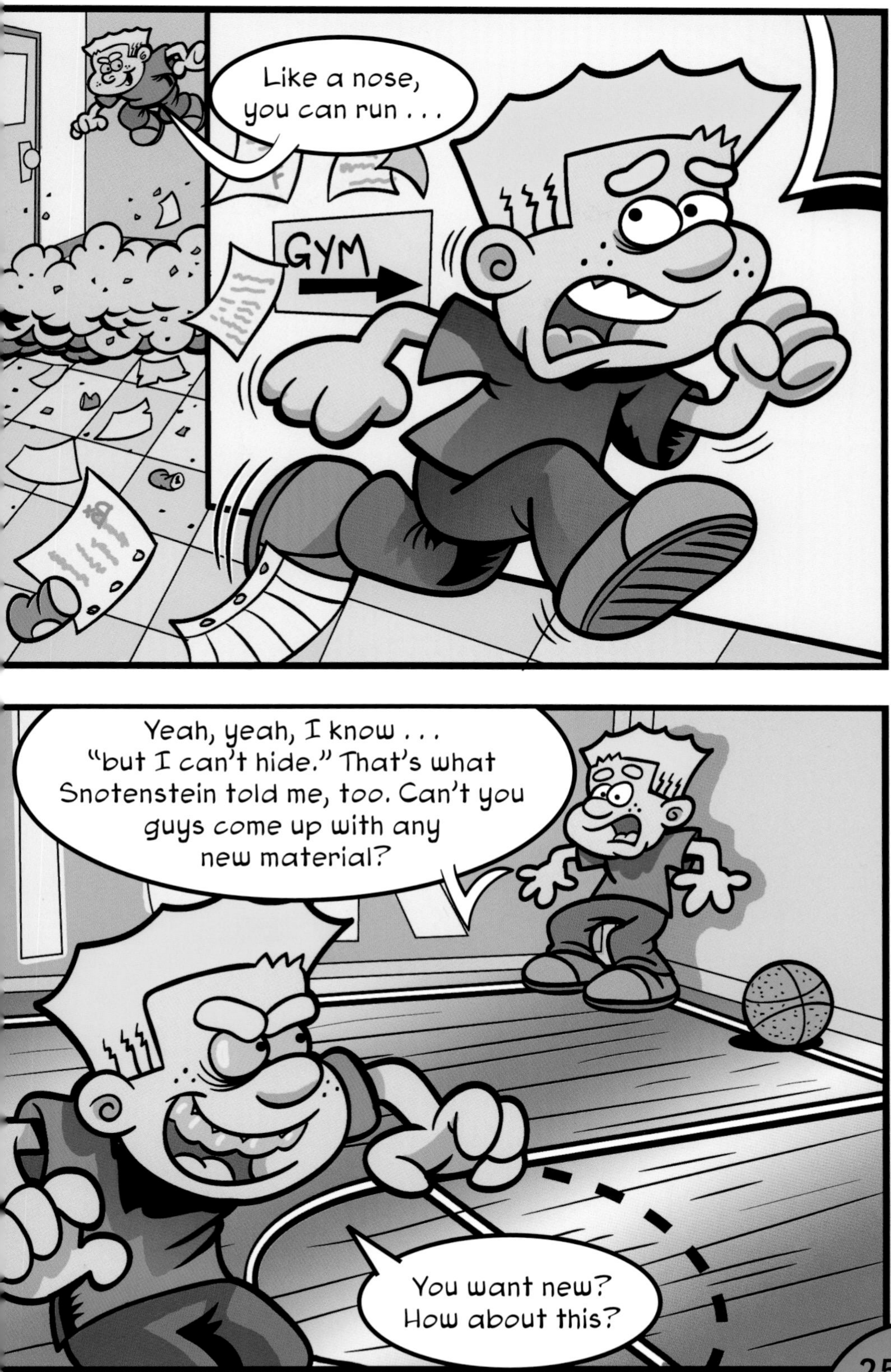

Like a nose, you can run . . .
GYM
Yeah, yeah, I know . . . "but I can't hide." That's what Snotenstein told me, too. Can't you guys come up with any new material?
You want new? How about this?

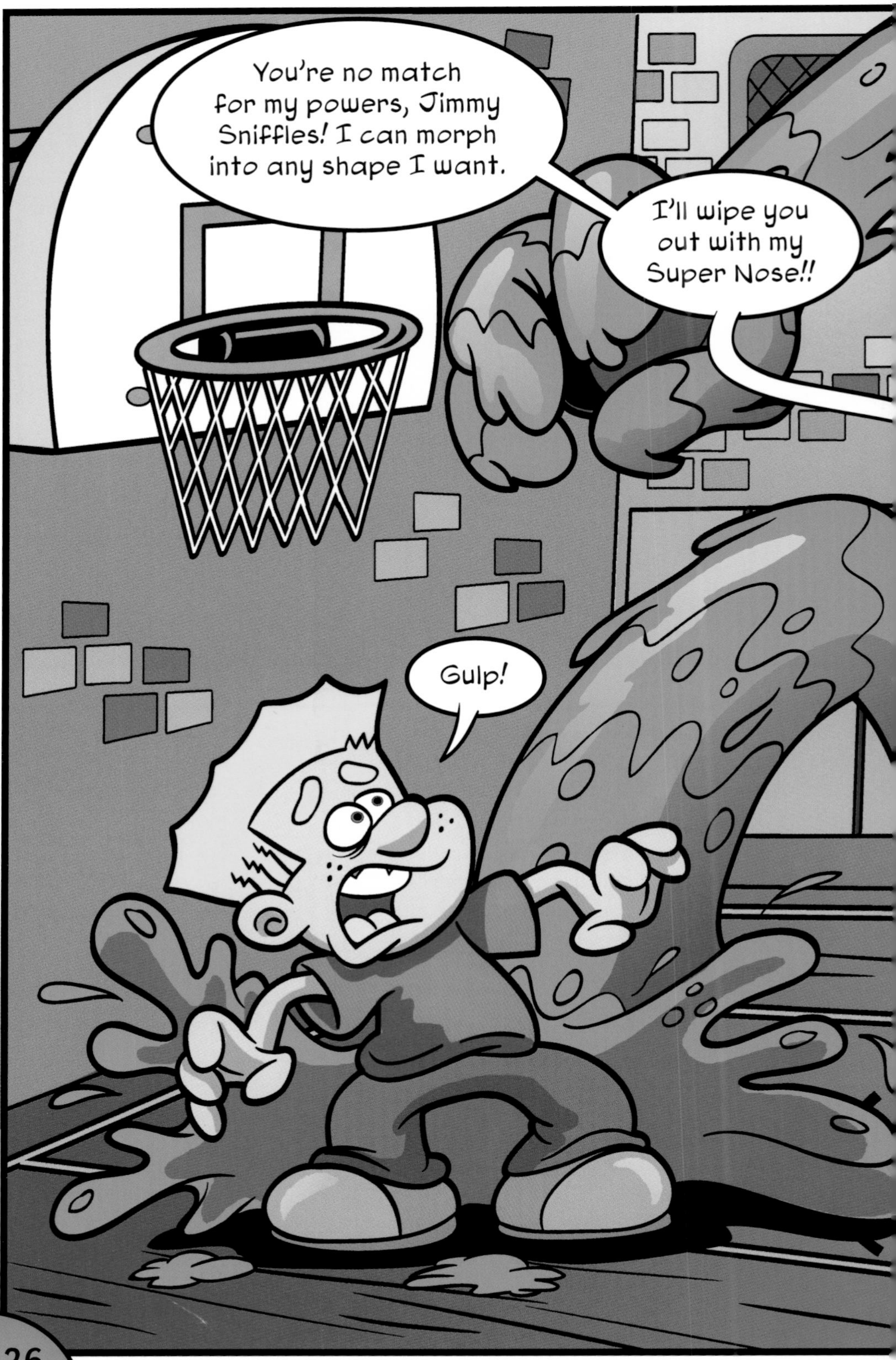
You're no match for my powers, Jimmy Sniffles! I can morph into any shape I want.
I'll wipe you out with my Super Nose!!
Gulp!

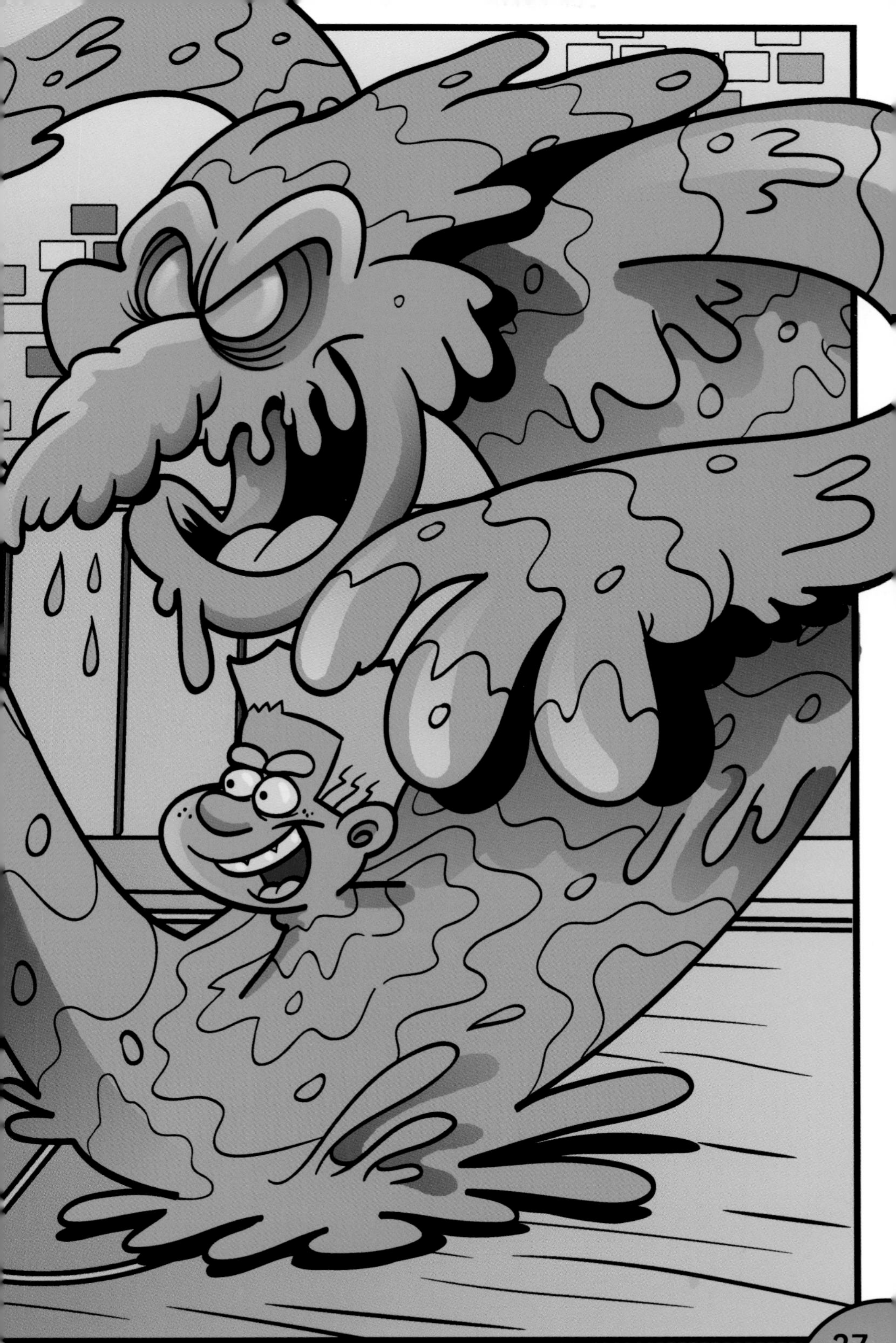

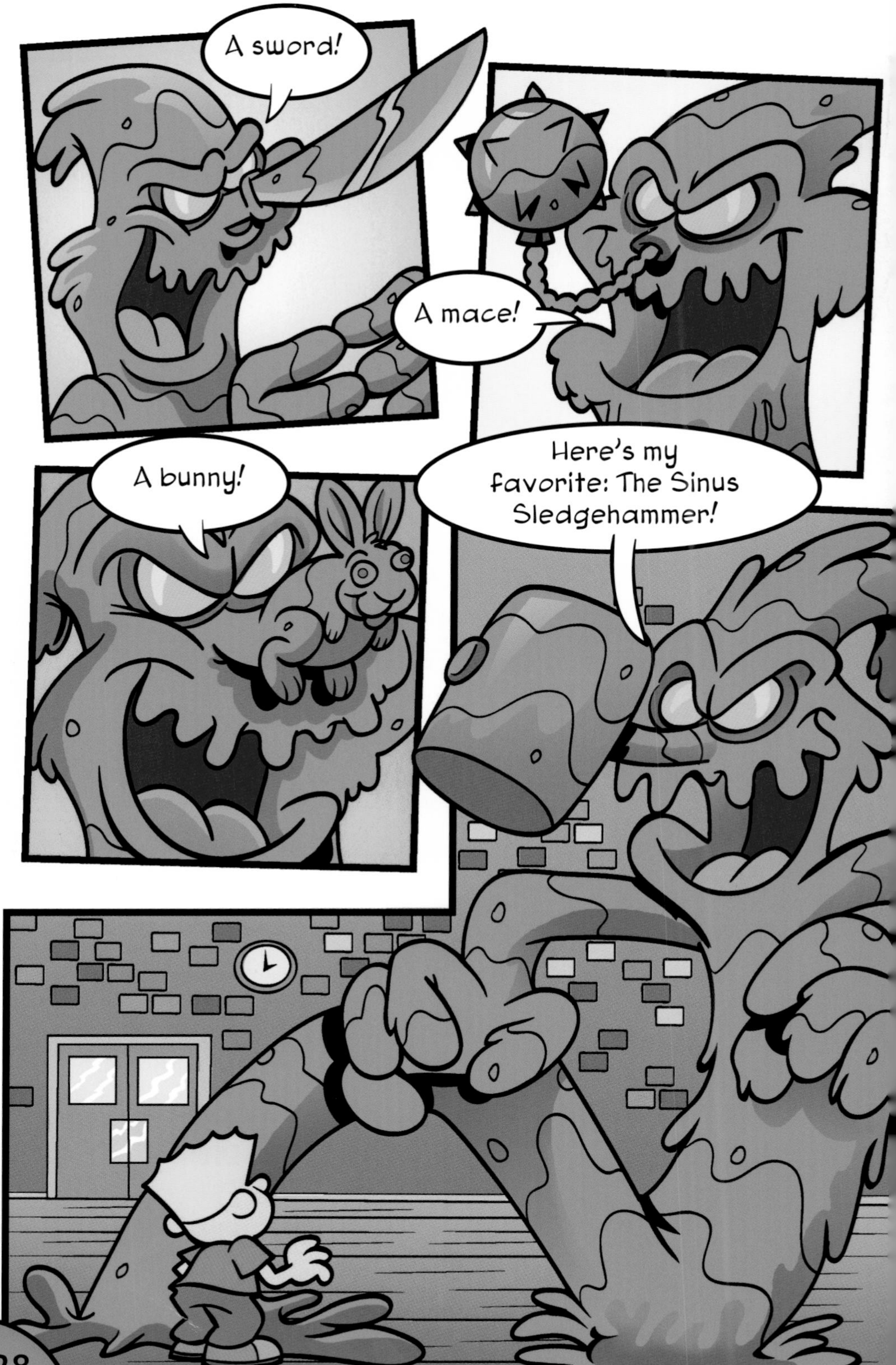
A sword!
A mace!
A bunny!
Here's my favorite: The Sinus Sledgehammer!

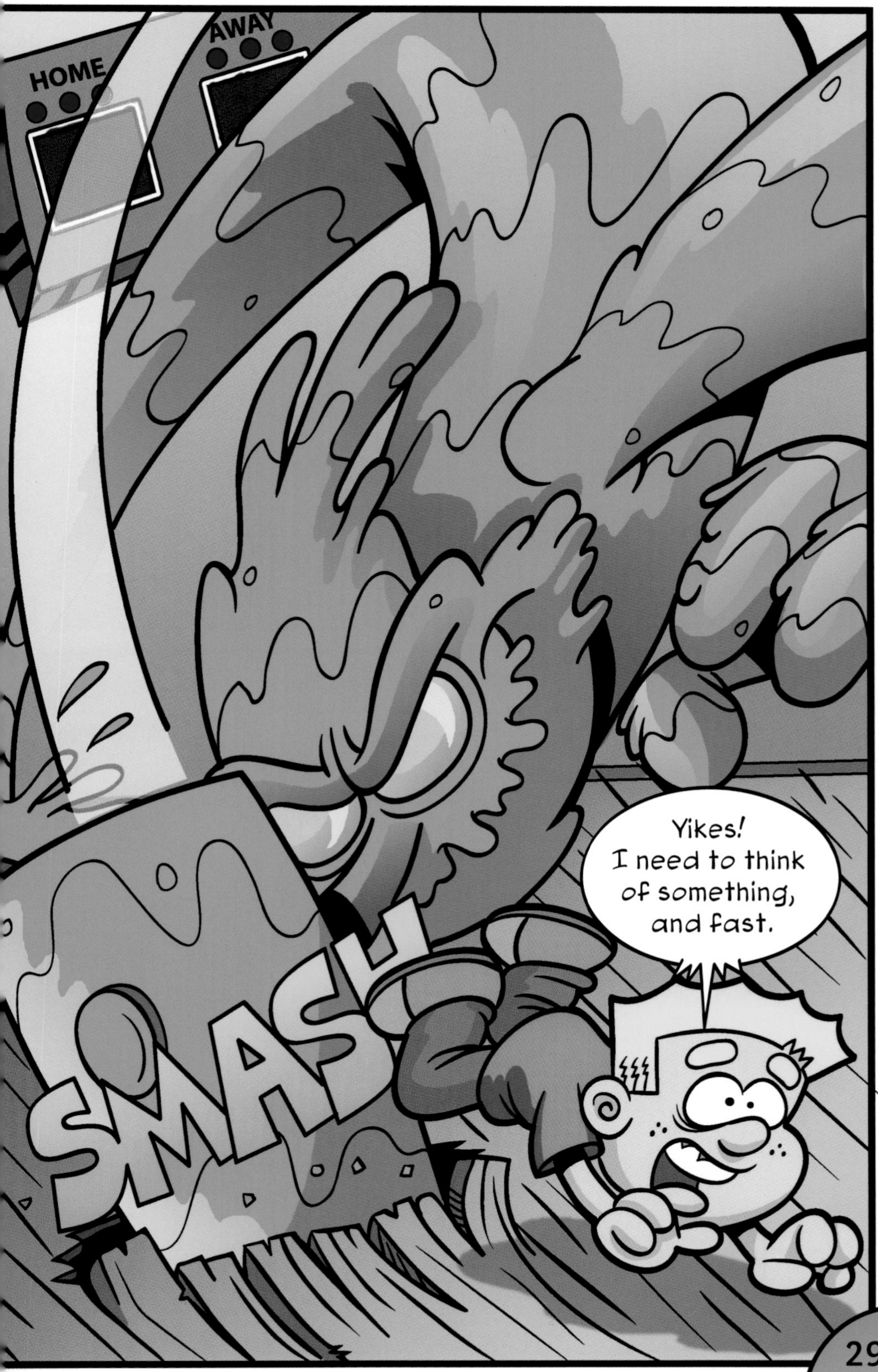
HOME
AWAY
SMASH
Yikes! I need to think of something, and fast.

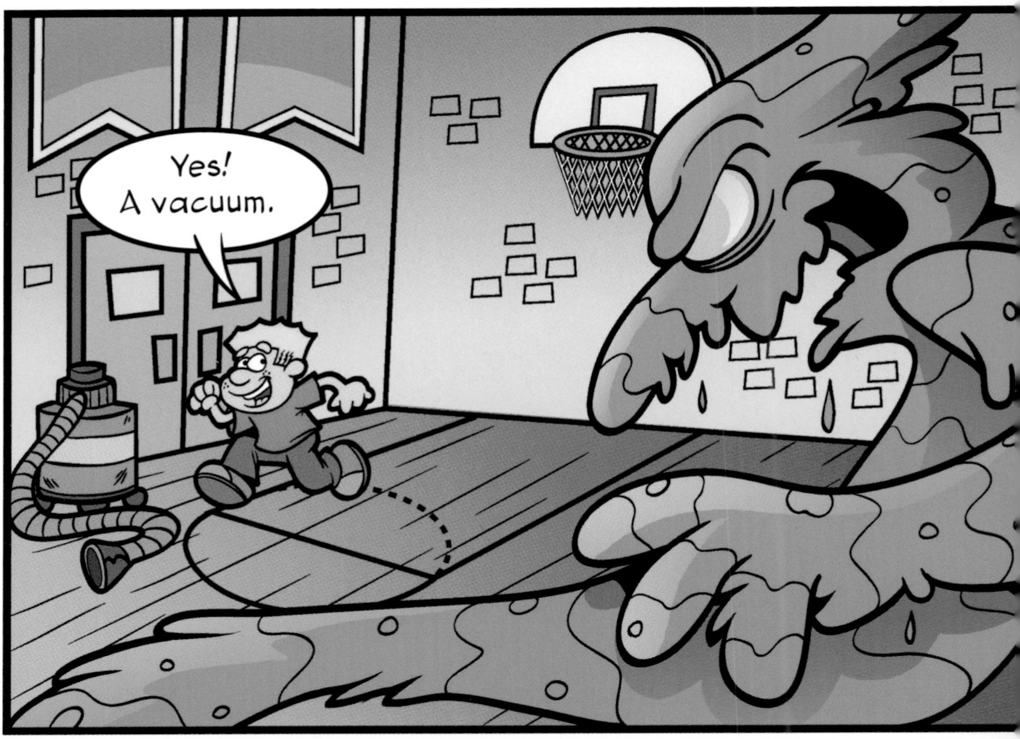
Yes!
A vacuum.

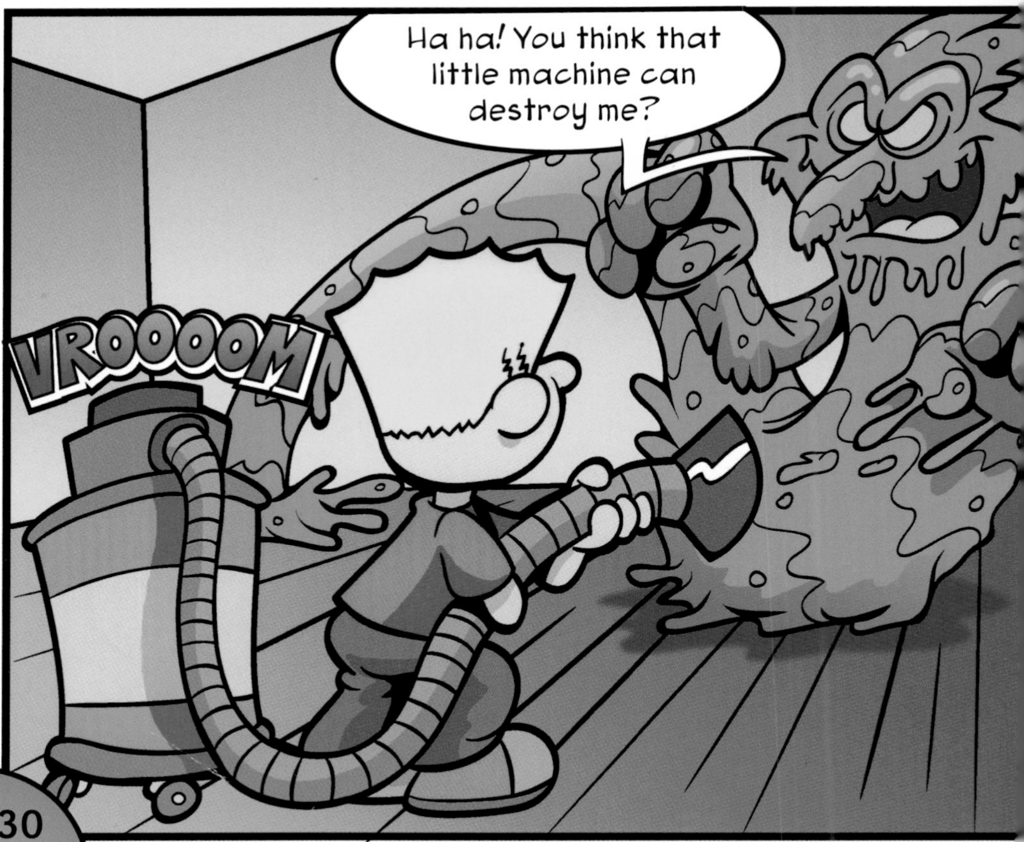
Ha ha! You think that little machine can destroy me?
VROOOOM

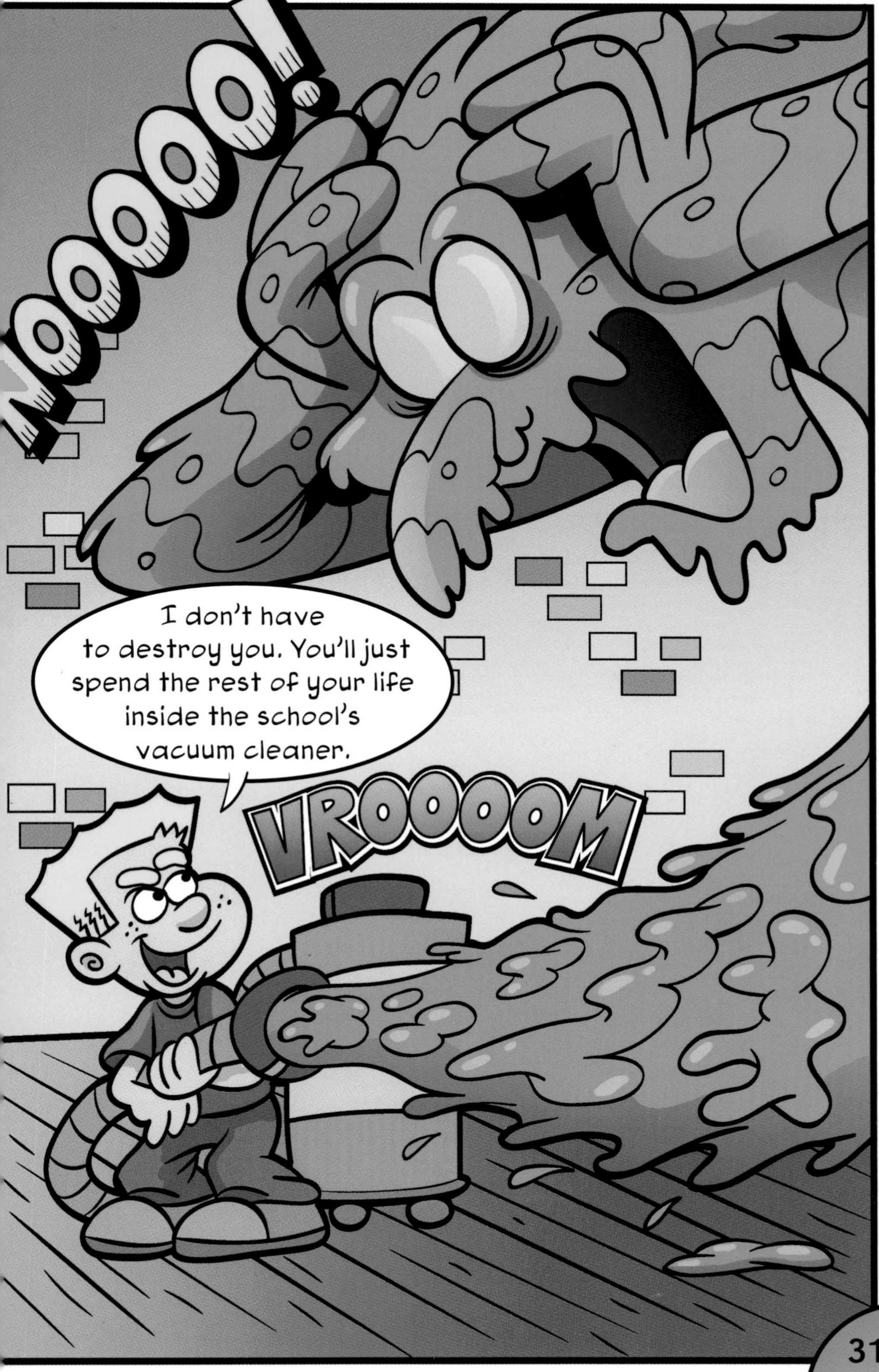
NOOOOOO!
I don't have to destroy you. You'll just spend the rest of your life inside the school's vacuum cleaner.
VROOOOM

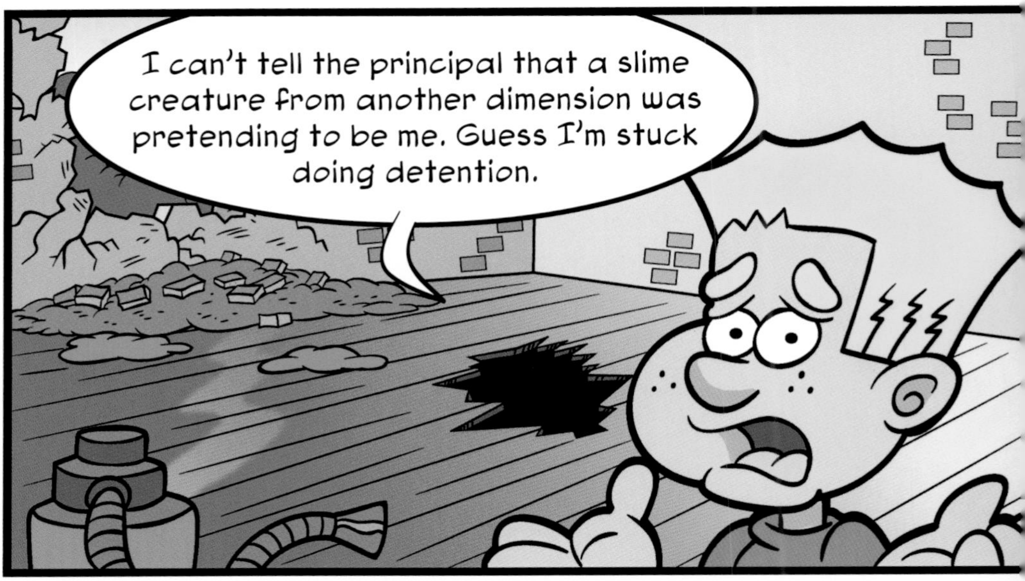
I can't tell the principal that a slime creature from another dimension was pretending to be me. Guess I'm stuck doing detention.

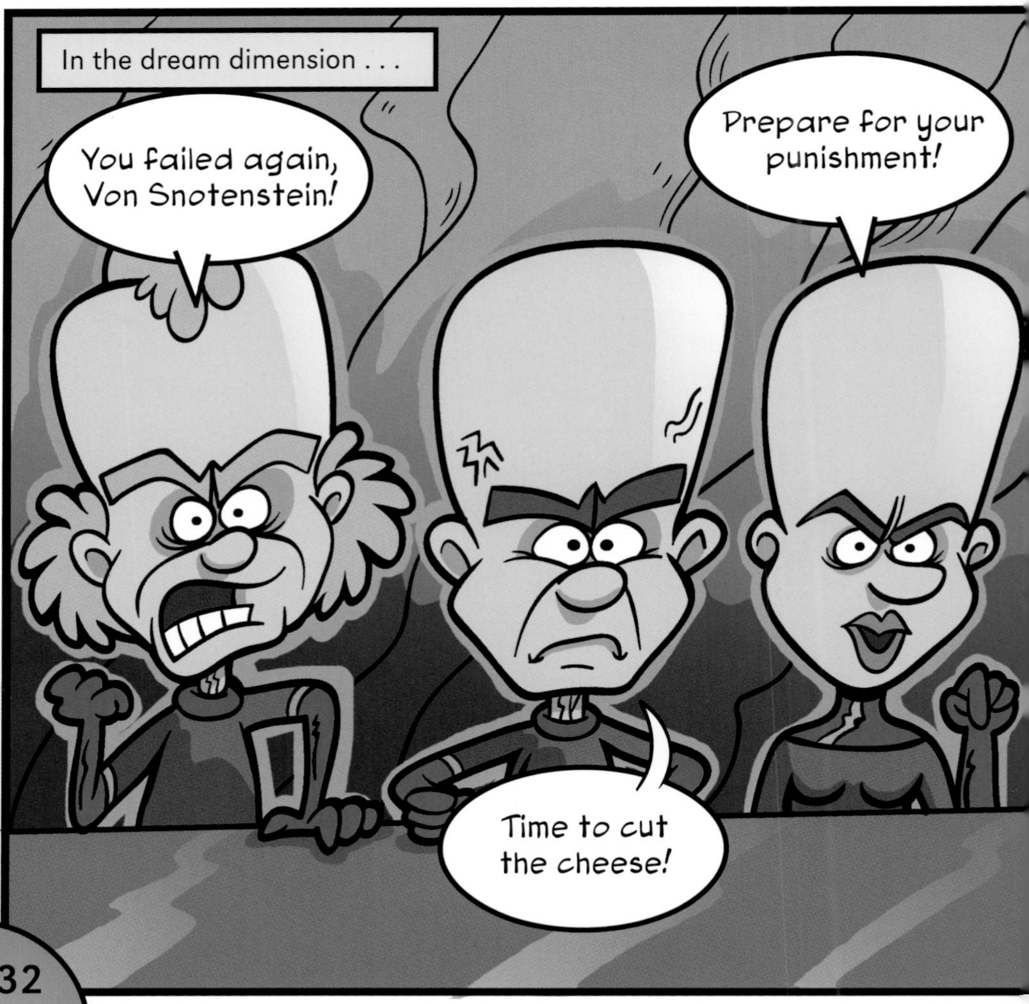
In the dream dimension . . .
You failed again, Von Snotenstein!
Prepare for your punishment!
Time to cut the cheese!

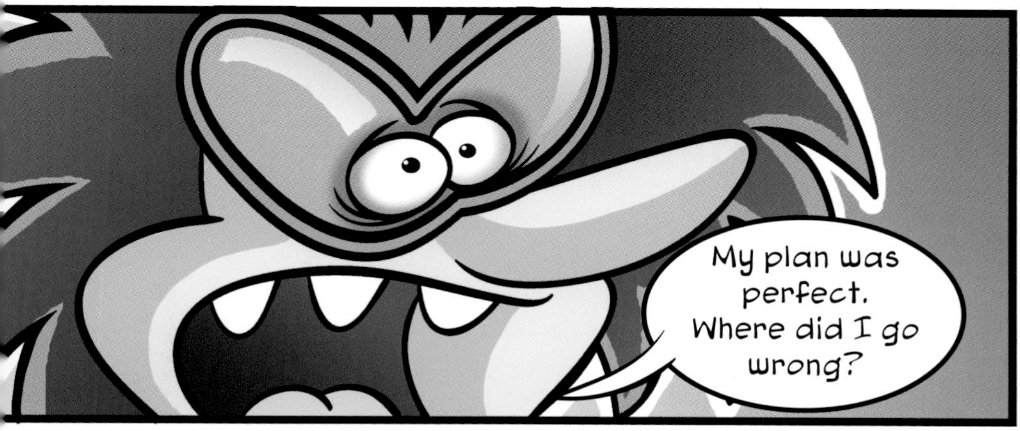
My plan was perfect. Where did I go wrong?

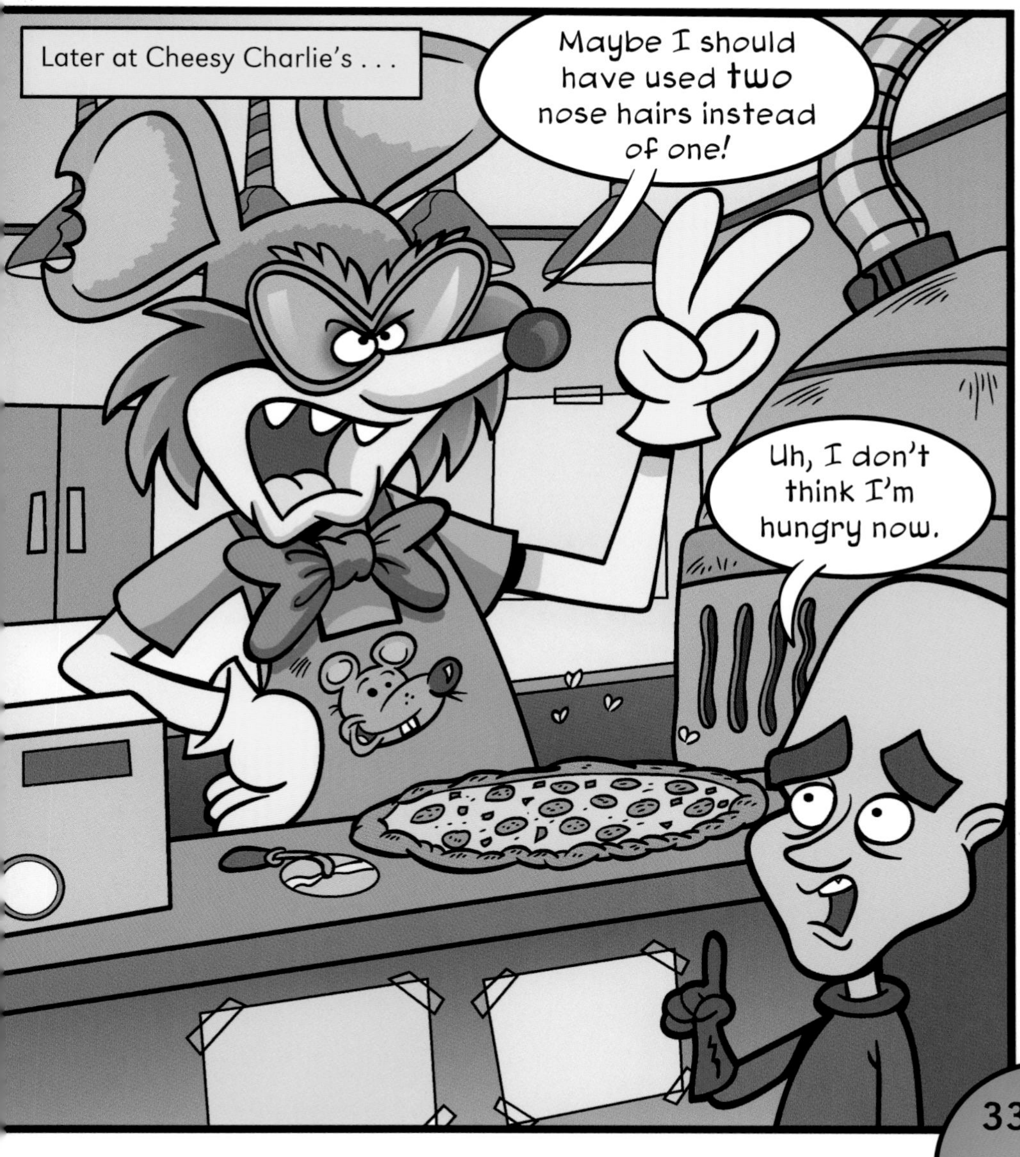
Later at Cheesy Charlie's . . .
Maybe I should have used two nose hairs instead of one!
Uh, I don't think I'm hungry now.

ABOUT THE AUTHOR

Born in 1962 in Denver, Colorado, Scott Nickel works by day at Paws, Inc., Jim Davis's famous Garfield studio, and he freelances by night. Burning the midnight oil, Scott has created hundreds of humorous greeting cards and written several children's books, short fiction for *Boys' Life* magazine, comic strips, and lots of really funny knock-knock jokes. He was raised in Southern California, but in 1995 Scott moved to Indiana, where he currently lives with his wife, two sons, six cats, and several sea monkeys.

ABOUT THE ILLUSTRATOR

Steve Harpster has loved drawing funny cartoons, mean monsters, and goofy gadgets since he was able to pick up a pencil. In first grade, instead of writing a report about a dog-sled story set in Alaska, Steve made a comic book about it. He was worried the teacher might not like it, but she hung it up for all the kids in the class to see. "It taught me to take a chance and try something different," says Steve. Steve landed a job drawing funny pictures for books. He used to be an animator for Disney. Now, Steve lives in Columbus, Ohio, with his wonderful wife, Karen, and their sheepdog, Doodle.

GLOSSARY

arcade (ar-KAYD)—a fun place in a store or shopping mall where you can play video games and funny sport games, and eat snacks. It's also a great place to give an evil villain detention.

detention (duh-TEN-shin)—a punishment for a student where they have to stay late after school. It can also mean other kinds of punishment, like coming to school early or working at a pizza arcade.

dimension (duh-MEN-shun)—an environment or surrounding where things live and move

morph (morf)—to change shape or turn into something else

nuisance (NOO-sunss)—a pest, a pain, a bother. A flea is a nuisance to a dog. A super hero is a nuisance to a villain.

sinus (SY-nis)—one of the small, hollow spaces in your head that are connected to your nose

THE TRUTH ABOUT TWINS

There are two kinds of twins, fraternal and identical. Fraternal twins are born at the same time, but look different from each other. Identical twins look exactly alike.

Do twins have the same fingerprints as each other? No! They might have some of the same patterns on their fingertips, but they have many more differences.

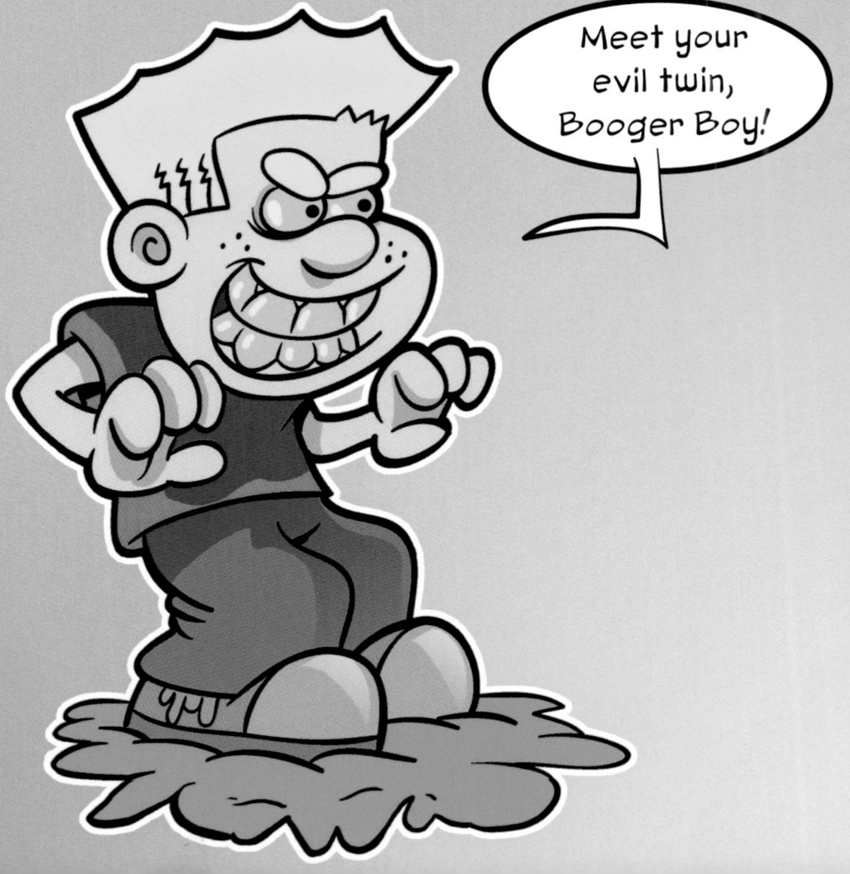
Meet your evil twin, Booger Boy!

The country of Nigeria in Africa has more twins than anywhere else in the world. One birth in every 22 is twins. The Nigerians think it is because they eat so many yams.

In the United States, there are more twins born in Massachusetts and Connecticut than in any other state. Maybe it has something to do with all those double letters in their names! Weird.

The talented Cirque Du Soleil circus likes to hire twins for their shows. They have had as many as 9 sets of twins performing in one show!

The world's most famous twins were Chang and Eng Bunker who were brothers from Siam (now known as Thailand). The two boys, born in 1811, were joined together at the chest. For a time, other conjoined twins were also known as "Siamese twins."

What the —? It's me. Only greener, and grosser!

DISCUSSION QUESTIONS

1. If you don't have a twin, would you like one? Would you like to be around someone who looks and acts just like you? Why or why not? If you **are** a twin, what is it like? What would life be like if you did **not** have a twin?

2. The evil Jimmy can turn his nose into anything! If you had that power, what would you turn your nose into and why?

3. Many kids would love to work at a place like Cheesy Charlie's Pizza Arcade. Why do you think Doctor von Snotenstein hates it so much?

WRITING PROMPTS

1. Who are those strange little people who tell Dr. von Snotenstein what he can and can't do? Are they aliens? Are they powerful? Do they like Jimmy Sniffles? Describe where you think they come from and what kind of lives they have.

2. The monster that Jimmy finally defeats is scared of being trapped in the vacuum cleaner. Inside will be all kinds of things sucked up from a school lunchroom. Yikes! Describe what the monster will find inside that disgusting vacuum bag.

3. After Jimmy defeats the evil twin creature, he needs to go back and explain to his principal what really happened. Will his principal believe him? Should Jimmy apologize to the students who were hurt by the evil Jimmy? Write down what you think happens after the story ends.

More cheese!

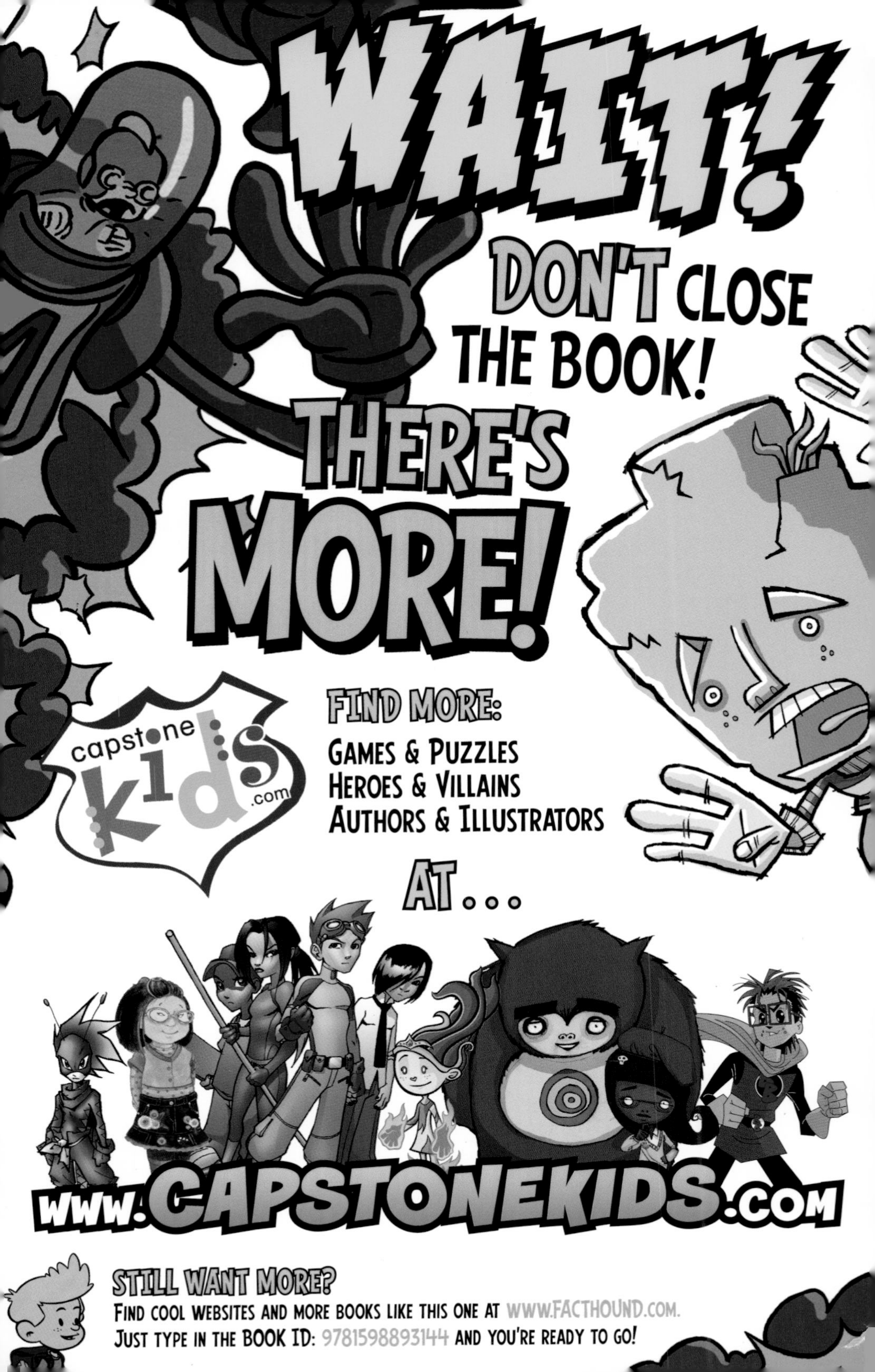
WAIT!
DON'T CLOSE THE BOOK!
THERE'S MORE!
capstone kids .com
FIND MORE:
GAMES & PUZZLES
HEROES & VILLAINS
AUTHORS & ILLUSTRATORS
AT...
WWW.CAPSTONEKIDS.COM
STILL WANT MORE?
FIND COOL WEBSITES AND MORE BOOKS LIKE THIS ONE AT WWW.FACTHOUND.COM.
JUST TYPE IN THE BOOK ID: 9781598893144 AND YOU'RE READY TO GO!